Desert Fate

Book 3
The Wolves of Twin Moon Ranch

by Anna Lowe

Contents

Other books in this series

visit www.annalowebooks.com

Free Book

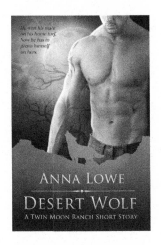

Desert Wolf

Get your free e-book now!

Sign up for my newsletter at *annalowebooks.com* to get your free copy of *Desert Wolf* (Book 1.1 in the series).

Lana Dixon may have won her destined mate's heart, but that was in Arizona. Now, she's bringing her desert wolf home to meet her family — the sworn enemies of his pack. How far will they push her mate to prove himself worthy? And is their relationship ready for the test?

Chapter One

Stefanie lay belly down in the dirt, vaguely aware of the first tap of sunlight upon her back. The wound on her neck throbbed, a reminder of the madman who set off this nightmare. The nightmare that had brought her to this place.

When she cracked one eye open, the red rock landscape was glowing orange-pink with dawn. She sucked in a long, unsteady breath, and it seemed like half of Arizona was squeezed into that lungful of air because her head spun. The place was like old leather: dry, worn, and rugged, yet rich and textured at the same time. Gritty and alive.

A little like her. Gritty. Alive, if only just.

She was going mad now, too, imagining all kinds of crazy things, like sprouting fur and claws and howling at the moon. Driving at breakneck speeds across two states hadn't helped outrun those crazy thoughts, nor had it shaken the feeling of being pursued.

Going to the police wasn't an option, much as she was tempted to try. If they heard the truth, they'd check her in to a mental ward. She could play it all out in her mind already.

What seems to be the problem, miss?

I was attacked.

The cop would nod, reach for a report, and wait for more.

I was attacked by a man with two-inch fangs who growled and grabbed me and—

That's when the officer would tear up his report, pick up the phone, and ask for the psych ward.

No, going to the cops was not an option.

She licked her lips, trying to assemble her scattered thoughts, but they all kept coming back to two words.

Skinwalker. Wolf.

Two words aimed at her not far past the Colorado-Arizona state line. She'd pulled over at a trading post after driving like a banshee for hours, desperately thirsty and bone tired. When had that been? Yesterday? The day before? She couldn't remember. Only that she'd made straight for the water fountain, hoping the shadows hid the mess she had become. Her hair, her clothes—all of them a mess. At least she'd had a shirt to change into. One that wasn't covered in blood.

She still wasn't sure how she'd survived after losing that much blood, but all that had mattered at that moment was the feel of cool water sliding down her throat. She barely caught the nod of greeting from the old Navajo woman who sat hunched over some beadwork in the shade—but she couldn't miss it when the woman suddenly jolted off her stool and backed away, her eyes wide in horror.

"Skinwalker..." The ancient voice rasped with fear.

Stefanie snapped away from the fountain and put her hands up in protest.

"Wolf..." the old woman murmured, clutching at her robe.

Stef stammered and stumbled until she was back in her car. Then she peeled out of the parking lot and sped away. But even as she drove—going sixty-five, seventy-five, pushing eighty—the words kept echoing in her mind.

Skinwalker. Wolf.

It was sunset—a few hours and several hundred miles later—before she'd calmed down enough to pull over. She'd stared at her knuckles, locked white around the wheel, then tilted her chin up to study the stars. That, she remembered exactly. The sky, blood red around the horizon, deep indigo overhead. The cool evening air. The rattle and whoosh of cars racing by. Where was she going? What would she do when she got there?

She traced the hook of the Big Dipper then the W of Cassiopeia with her eyes. For all that had gone wrong in the past few days, the stars looked exactly right tonight.

Then she did a double take. Wait. Hadn't they looked better from about a mile back?

2

I am definitely losing my mind.

No one could sense that small a change. But there was a hush in the air that stopped her from shaking the idea away. Like the desert had whispered something and was waiting for her response.

Something like, *That is the way you must go.*

So, okay, she made the U-turn. If instinct told her to follow the stars, she'd follow the stars, no matter how crazy it seemed. What else did she have to lose?

A mile later, an unmarked road split away from the highway and an upward glance told her that the stars really did look better from here, if still not exactly right. So she bumped down the dirt road, checking the stars every few minutes.

They did look better from this angle, part of her insisted, and for a little while, that part took over. Every mile she drove took her closer to...

To where?

To wherever it was that felt right. It was like a blindfolded childhood game where you honed in on something: warmer, warmer...

Then the right front tire blew out and hissed its anger into the night. She groaned, dropped her forehead to the steering wheel, and stayed there a long time.

No one could help her, not even the cops. And now, she was stranded in the middle of nowhere in the middle of the night. How could she have thought there was anything right about this?

A coyote yipped in the distance then broke into a long, warbling howl. For a minute, it sounded vaguely... familiar. So much that she was almost tempted to sing along. Tempted to toss her head back and let out all the frustration, the pain, the fear. To disappear into the desert and hide in a den.

When the coyote trailed off, loneliness came crushing in along with the crazy images that had started plaguing her at night. Images of running into the night like a wild thing. Of howling her sorrow to the moon through a long, pointed snout. Of tearing something fleshy apart and tasting warm, sweet blood...

She fumbled with the door handle and jumped out of the car as if that were the seat of her madness, and then rushed into the shadows of the desert. Faster and faster until all she heard were her own hurried breaths, her own desperate footfalls.

It all became a blur until dawn, when she found herself belly down in the dirt, the sun tapping on her back. There was a rattle, and she glanced up in time to see the diamond pattern of a snake slithering by. Had he too, spent a frigid night on this mesa?

She was still flopped there, vaguely aware of the intensifying heat of morning, when an engine grumbled in the distance—the first vehicle to pass since last night.

Maybe they can help! Part of her wanted to believe that impossibility.

No one can help, the other part cried. *No one can understand.*

A good thing she was far enough into the bush that the driver wouldn't see her. She'd be left in peace, hopefully to die.

I don't want to die!

But some things were worse than death, so she lay still. If she was lucky, the sun would take care of what the snake failed to do. All she had to do was lie there and let her mind drift.

She should have known not to step foot on that Colorado ranch alone. Should have listened to the creeping doubts that had warned her away...

The cool earth under her cheek carried a vibration. Something was moving nearby.

A shadow fell over her, too tall for a snake or coyote, and she tensed. The touch on her shoulder was warm and broad. A human hand. With it came a human voice.

"Are you okay?"

The voice deep and warm, and she wouldn't have minded listening to it all day.

But the cynic in her wanted to snort. Okay? She'd nearly had her throat ripped out by a maniac. Her dreams were nightmares full of canine sights and sounds. She'd been on the run for days. Okay?

I've never been further from okay.

Adrenaline coursed through her veins as the instinct to flee kicked in. With a lunge and a twist, she was up and running, crashing through the bush.

"Hey! Wait!" the man's voice, so soft a moment ago, shouted in surprise.

Like hell, she was waiting. She squinted as she ran, trying to adjust to the bright sunlight. Despite the stranger on her heels, running gave her a thrill, like that of a captive animal set free. She darted around a cactus, hammered up a slope, then skidded down the other side in huge leaps. But the air rushed behind her, and with it came the jolt of a flying tackle. Then she was tumbling and tangling with her attacker, both of them bashing into the hillside until they ground out against a rock.

"Ooof." The man groaned, then cursed. "Lady..." he started, then suddenly stopped.

He had her pinned on her back under his sheer weight. All she could see against the glare of the sun was his outline. It didn't take much for her imagination to fill in the features of a different attacker, a different man.

"No! Get off me! Stop!" She clawed at him wildly, trying to break away. She wouldn't let Ron get close! Wouldn't let him bite her again!

He pushed her back into the ground, hands firm yet careful. Confident. Controlled.

"It's okay. Listen, it's okay."

The voice was low and gritty, and that's when she realized that this wasn't Ron. This man stood much, much higher up the food chain. He was stronger. Smarter. Faster. A predator, not a scavenger like Ron. She could tell by the firm line of his mouth, the clear honesty of his eyes. The brightest pair of eyes she'd ever seen: summer blue shot with strands of gold, like the sun streaming through a cloud on the leading edge of a rainstorm. She found herself going warm all over, lost in the allure of that light.

If this was death—hell, she'd greet it like an old friend.

5

Chapter Two

The minute Kyle saw the wild flecks of color in the woman's eyes, he knew. The question was, what the hell was he going to do with a Changeling like her?

He'd been sitting on his porch, wondering how he was going fill an entire week off work, when he spotted a pair of hawks circling the mesa. They weren't circling high in the usual way, but dipping and swooping as if coming in for a closer look.

A closer look at what?

So he'd driven out, then hiked into the hills to see for himself, and found a woman. One who'd sprung off the ground like a corpse come alive and sprinted like a deer for the horizon. It had taken everything he had to catch her.

Why did he chase her? Because the law enforcement officer in him never really went off duty. Because anyone who fled must be guilty of something.

Because something deep inside him said, *Catch that woman. Catch her now.*

When he finally caught up and flipped her around to face the light, he'd expected a drugged-out glare, a string of obscenities.

He hadn't been expecting *this*.

Tousled hair, wild eyes. Honey-brown eyes lit with irregular bolts of gold, green, and gray. A sure sign, he knew, of trouble. For her, for him, for his whole pack. Where had this she-wolf come from? And Jesus, where had she learned to fight? It was all he could do to keep her pinned.

He sniffed, searching for the telltale odor of a human recently turned, already thinking ahead to questioning—until her scent set off a rushing sensation. A trickle of heat joined another and another until they formed a torrent and his whole system was engulfed by her scent. The sunlight dimmed and everything became the warmth pulling him in. The next thing he knew, he was right up against her neck, all but licking her skin. Inhaling her. His nose traced a long, lingering line along her neck and up to her ear. Her scent was foreign, yet familiar. Dangerous yet enticing, like a new kind of spice.

Want. More. Closer, his wolf demanded. *Now.*

She tipped her head back, drawing him in, and Kyle followed. Everything tuned out until all that remained was the tingle of her body beneath his. Her fingers went from clawing to threading through his, and the whole world seemed to hum and throb. His hip brushed her thigh and a growl built inside him. A hunger. It felt like his heart was trying to get closer to her by climbing straight over his lungs. He slid along her body and let their jaws scrape, their breath cross and—

With a snap, he jerked away, breath ragged. He blinked, trying to pull his senses out of their wild spin. Whoa. What the hell was he doing?

Touching. Tasting. Liking, his wolf growled.

His canines fought to extend past his gums with the instinct to claim, but he clamped his jaws together to lock them away.

"Look, I..."

He tried to catch his breath, to blurt out an apology—anything!—but the words all stuck in his throat. What the hell was wrong with him? He'd worked dozens of assault cases, put countless sick bastards away—and yet there he was, pinning a woman down. He'd explored her like a man in a brothel, not an officer of the law. No wonder she had that wild look in her eye.

The woman heaved a sharp breath, and the soft welcome of her body went steel-hard as she, too, snapped to some realization and shoved an angry palm against his chest. The kaleidoscope eyes that had drawn him in went from dazed to outraged.

"Get off me!"

He dragged himself back and held up both hands. "Sorry! I mean..."

She leaped to her feet and immediately swayed, her shoulder-length hair echoing the movement. When he put out an arm to steady her, the tingling started again. What was it with this woman? He'd never encountered a Changeling before—well, except himself, but that was all a dim memory now. Maybe Changelings created their own high-voltage force fields. What did he know?

"Are you okay?"

"I'm fine," she snapped, batting his arm away.

Right. He slipped closer as she swayed and ended up clutching his arm for balance. He tried to keep his grip tight enough to steady her but loose enough not to be a threat. "Why did you run?"

"Why did you?" she shot back and promptly closed her eyes on what looked like a wave of nausea.

Better not to go there. Not now. "Can you make it to my car? I've got water there."

She looked tattered and worn, like her khaki shorts and the scratched legs that extended out of them. The very long, slender legs. Her purple T-shirt was so covered in dust and burrs, it took him a minute to make out the logo. There was a silhouette of a mountain ridge with the words *Boulder Marathon* fit in among the peaks.

No wonder the woman could run.

"Just leave me alone," she said, though her fingers were gripping him tight.

"You need help."

"I need to be left alone."

A memory kicked toward the surface from the depths of his memory. He'd said exactly those words when he first came to Twin Moon Ranch. Lucky no one had heeded him.

"Believe me, you need help."

"No one can help me."

He took in her matted hair, the dark lines under her eyes, and wondered how long she'd been on the run. He took a deep breath, reminding himself not to get too involved. He had to do a lot of that in his job. Usually, he could tune out, step back. But this time, his wolf was stirring, his nostrils flaring to catch more of that alluring scent.

He leaned in with a whisper. "I know what you are."

He saw her eyes go wide and her body stiffen, though she tried to strike a nonchalant pose. She was proud, that was clear. Reluctant to show weakness. He knew the type; saw it in the mirror a couple of times a day. Or at least, the few times he bothered looking.

"And what am I?"

He looked at the colors swirling in her eyes, the inner wolf begging for release.

"You're the same as me."

Or what he'd once been; close enough. He'd made it through the Changeling stage and out the other side, becoming a true shifter, capable of changing from his human body to wolf and back.

He could see her weighing believing against fleeing and wished he could explain. Every human carried a second side deep inside, and hers had been awakened. If only he could just say it. *Changeling.*

But words would never convince her, so he held his tongue, afraid to spook her off. More afraid than he ought to be. Why did it matter so much?

It matters, his wolf growled.

Slowly, carefully, she reached a hand toward him. The woman had guts, that was for sure. He held his breath when she touched a single finger to his jaw, and the rush came again. Whatever strange energy she carried had jumped over to him and was spinning crazy laps around his body.

She tilted his chin up, examining his neck. A second later, she pulled away with an angry cluck.

"I don't think we're talking about the same thing."

"We're the same," he insisted. It's just that his neck wasn't where he carried his scars.

The woman watched, wary, as he worked down the top buttons of his shirt and pulled one side toward his shoulder, exposing the four parallel scars. Claw marks, puckered and red even after all these years.

"A bite's not the only way to turn someone," he explained, keeping his voice steady even as memories roiled inside.

She stared, first at the scars, then at his face.

"Wolf?" she whispered.

He nodded, letting out a puff of relief. At least she hadn't turned tail and run again.

"There's someone we need to see. Someone who can help," he said, tilting his head in the direction of his truck.

"How can anyone help?" The hopelessness in her tone made him ache.

He ran a hand through his hair; the sweat was already making it go stiff. What the hell should he tell her?

"I don't know. But I know they can." Somehow. He nodded toward the truck, wondering if she would follow.

But the woman had gone stock-still, gaping at him. What had he said? Kyle tensed, ready to grab her if she tried to flee again.

She didn't run, though. In fact, she took a step closer, eyes swirling like a witch's brew.

"It's you," she murmured, lifting a hand as if to touch his face.

He blinked, wondering if maybe she was on drugs, after all.

She nodded, a look of wonder replacing the raw distrust on her face. "It is you. Kyle. Kyle Williams."

He rocked back on his heels, unsure what to make of this stranger who knew his name. Then something in his memory gave a sleepy lurch, and just like that, the woman wasn't a stranger anymore. The freckles, the tousled hair, those eyes... Take away the glimmering flecks, and the hickory color was one in a million. A melody kicked off in his mind, and there she was, his brown-eyed girl.

"Stef," he managed. "Stefanie Alt." He gaped a minute longer, trying to process it all. "What are you doing here?"

Her eyes asked him the same thing.

Chapter Three

Stefanie sucked in a long breath. She'd always had to do that around Kyle: take a deep breath and feign normality. Something about the hulk of him did that to her, even when he was fourteen and nowhere near the man he was now.

Because Kyle Williams, erstwhile neighbor and troubled kid on the block, had filled out quite nicely since those days when they were both army brats living side by side in family housing. Quite nicely, indeed, judging by the layers of steel she'd been pushing against a moment ago. But the underlying parts she'd always had X-ray vision for were unchanged. Where others saw leather-tough, Stef saw battered and bruised. Where others saw a time bomb, ready to explode, she saw raw nerves. Where others heard only silence, she heard a soul begging for help.

She remembered it all too well: the shouts, the cries, the drunken threats of Kyle's stepfather. The helplessness they'd both felt. The army had a way of hiding its own dirty laundry, and nobody ever got serious about trying to help.

She looked up and down the six-foot frame, comparing it to the lanky kid of her memory. He had been a grade ahead of her in school—should have been two, but he'd repeated a year somewhere along the line—and yet every time they passed in the hallway or made eye contact in the cafeteria, she felt like she had a friend. His hair was short and spiky as always, as if it was part of his defenses. The narrow mouth, the impossibly blue eyes.

"Kyle..." There was no mistaking him, for all that time had added creases to his face. The guarded expression was the same, too. The man, like the boy, held his cards close to his chest.

"Stef..."

He remembered, too. Maybe even more than her name, given the way those eyes were flashing with memories. What was he thinking, seeing her reduced to such a mess?

A yucca swayed in the wind, triggering something inside her to scream caution. Just because they'd once been friends didn't mean he was the same old Kyle. He'd chased her down, after all, and thrown her to the dirt. Could he be trusted?

Yes.

The word resounded deep inside her lungs and spread through her body like a blue flame.

Yes.

She could trust Kyle the way she'd trusted him back then, the day he'd found her crying on her very first day of school. Her fifth school, and it was only seventh grade. You'd think that a girl with that much experience picking up and starting over would have gotten over the ripped-open feel of it all, but no. Once the see-how-tough-I-am energy she'd been channeling all day wore off, tears had taken over and her mind chanted one wish: that home could be a place to move to for more than twelve months. A place to stay. Forever.

"Stef," he breathed, blue eyes searching as they'd done that very first time.

She had already gone from outrage to shock and warm recognition; now she skipped ahead to shy. To Kyle, she was probably still just the awkward girl from next door. The two of them had only had that one year in Fort Benning in common, and she was the forgettable type with plain brown hair and brown eyes. The kind who never quite fit in.

A little like Kyle. Except he was anything but forgettable.

"What are you doing here?" he asked. The words fast-forwarded her into the present. There they were, the two of them, standing in the desert. Here. Now. Close.

Close enough to see the pulse in his neck. Close enough to inhale his warm scent.

Close enough to kiss.

14

She forced herself to snap back to the question. What was she doing in Arizona? Her adrenaline high collapsed on top of itself, leaving her sagging.

"I wish I knew."

Kyle's eyes went liquid, twin icebergs melting into puddles of achingly bright blue. He reached for her arm. "How about a drink?"

She hesitated, still reeling from it all: his sudden appearance, running away, getting tackled. And most of all, what had happened next. The way he came down over her was way too... intimate. For a few seconds, everything had vanished— the desert, the fear, the pain—and it was only him. She'd clung to his arms like a shipwrecked sailor to a piece of flotsam, praying for salvation.

The crazy thing was, he'd been the same. One minute he'd been sniffing her, like... like he *wanted* her, and the next, he was pulling back with shock written all over his face. And the worst part was, she'd wanted him, too. Wanted to hold him, feel him, *have* him. If he'd held her a second longer, she'd have thrown a leg around him like a dog in heat. Jesus, what had come over her?

"You sure you're okay?"

"Fine."

Sunstroke, maybe? Or was the madness progressing? Now she wasn't just dreaming of becoming a beast, but behaving like one, too. Soon she'd be lusting after any whiff of testosterone that came her way. She shook her head, disgusted. But what to do?

"Come on. Come get a drink." His voice was an addiction waiting to happen, and she was all too eager to try her first hit.

So she followed him down the slope, trying not to notice how neatly those cargo pants boxed his ass or how wide his T-shirt stretched across his shoulders.

"Jesus, Kyle. How long has it been?"

He glanced back at her, eyes guarded. "Fifteen years? Sixteen?"

Sixteen years. Surely sixteen years made him a stranger and not a friend.

But there he stood, holding the truck door open, looking all the world like a friend.

Stef hesitated then stepped forward and heaved herself into the cab. The door closing behind her only registered as a distant thump as she twisted the cap off the bottle on the seat and downed the tepid water in one desperate gulp.

She wiped the spillover from her chin when Kyle slid into the driver's seat. He sat quietly for a minute, looking at her. His eyebrows were angled up toward his ears, twin accent marks above the blue eyes.

"Stefanie," he murmured. The way it rolled off his tongue made her think of a bear licking honey. Long, sweet, satisfied, and more than willing to sample a little more. She slid him a sideways glance, but he started the truck and kept his eyes on the road. He headed away from the highway, not toward it. She wasn't sure what to make of that, but with a cooling breeze coming in through the window and a country tune playing on the radio, she didn't much care.

"Who do I need to see, Kyle?"

"Hmm?" He looked at her, and there they were again, those sky blue eyes—minus the streaks of gold. Had she been imagining that special effect? Well, she hadn't been imagining the rest. The square jaw, the parentheses around his mouth, the slanting cheekbones. He had the aura of an off-duty soldier or the veteran of one too many campaigns. A soldier of fortune, she wondered, or an honorable soul?

A man with a dark past, that much was certain. He'd been an enigma back then, and life had obviously swung a few more punches in his adulthood.

A lot like her.

"This is the way to my place." He must have sensed her tense up because he went on quickly. "You need something to eat, I figure, and a chance to clean up. Then I'll take you to the ranch."

Stefanie glanced in the side view mirror and blanched. No wonder he'd been eyeing her strangely. Her hair—never her strong suit—was sticking up on one side, matted on the other. God, she looked like a ghost. Her face was thinner, the hollows of her cheeks darker. She felt like a ghost, too. Her old life—her normal life—seemed so far away. How many days had it been since she'd fled Colorado? Four? Five?

"Is today... Thursday?"

He looked at her sharply. "Sunday. The twelfth."

She bit back her protest. How could it be Sunday? That made three days she couldn't account for, plus the couple she'd rather forget.

Kyle seemed more comfortable with silence than she was, so she let her eyes rove the truck, the scenery; anything but him. But after bouncing along on the dirt road for another few minutes, her thoughts took on the quality of the scenery: a distant blur, rushing by with no particular focal point. Arizona was like the truth—harsh and inescapable. Impossible to digest in one bite.

She tried focusing on a closer point. There was an ID card sitting on the console, and she could just make out the print: *Department of Public Safety.* She cast a sideways glance at Kyle. State Trooper? Wouldn't surprise her one bit. The eyes in the photo promised justice, hard justice, for anyone who dared victimize another. Even squeezed into a small square, the face in that picture was imposing. Almost as imposing as in real life.

You wanted a cop, she thought. *You got one.*

It could have been minutes or hours that they drove in silence. She barely noticed until her chin snapped up—along with her drooping eyelids. The truck slowed, approaching a house. His house?

She couldn't help but noticing, as she did with all buildings, the angle and orientation of the roof, part of her mind already calculating how many solar panels she might squeeze in, how many amps they might produce. A reminder that she had to call in to work. But how would she ever explain her long absence?

She shoved the worry aside. There was enough to deal with for now.

17

A porch ran across the face of the low-slung ranch house worn ragged by the elements. The place had a certain charm, though. It was a survivor, like Kyle. She followed him up the creaky stairs. In one corner of the porch was a box of recyclables with cobwebs strung between them. At the other end, a single chair was pulled up to the railing, staring blindly at the view. East, she noted, taking in the sloping lines of open scrubland beyond. Did he sit there and contemplate the cruelties life could deliver, or the joys?

"Hungry?" Kyle asked, pulling the screen door open with a rusty screech.

Starving, her stomach answered.

"I'm fine," she said.

He raised an eyebrow, and the accent mark stretched. "I remember that."

She crossed her arms. "Remember what?"

His thin smile grew. "That."

Stef wondered what exactly "that" meant to him. Her stubbornness? That's what her mother used to call it. She herself preferred doggedness, as a track coach once said.

The way his eyes wandered over her frame suggested it was something altogether different.

"What?"

He flashed a full smile, exposing a line of perfect teeth. "That. That..." He circled a hand in front of her body. "That tough guy act."

"Not an act, Williams." She did her best to bristle, though her heart wasn't in it.

Kyle looked at her, long and silent, then jutted his chin left. Like so much about him, that little gesture, that I'll-shelve-this-for-now movement, hadn't changed one bit.

He held the front door open for her—unlocked, she noticed—and waited as she wavered under the upside-down horseshoe hanging over the threshold. The inside of the house was dim, and her next steps felt terribly important, as if she were at a major crossroads instead of a tiny bump.

"Stef," he prompted, coaxing her in.

Chapter Four

She swallowed away her fears, stepped in, and blinked. The front room was small but homey. Clean but cluttered.

"It's, um...kind of a mess," he started, darting ahead to grab a pizza box and an empty bottle of beer.

Not that she'd been expecting neat, of course. Not with Kyle.

For the first time in a week, she smiled. "It's fine."

Books and magazines spilled over the ends of rough shelves balanced on cinder blocks. One wall was decorated with still-life paintings of desert flowers; the other held a drooping state map. The plaid couch practically patted her over to take a seat. A battered leather recliner hunched like a bulldog beside it, facing a stone fireplace. She could picture Kyle there, feet propped up, staring into the flames on a lonely winter night. All in all, the place was a strange cross between a bachelor pad and an old widow's nest, as if the former occupant had never quite moved out, and Kyle had never quite moved in.

He was already in the kitchen, rooting around the antique refrigerator, and just like that, she gave in to his quiet insistence.

By the time he led her out of the house an hour later, Kyle had not only fed and watered her like a hungry camel but also shooed her into the shower. Hot water and soap helped make her feel more... human, even if slipping into the clean shirt he'd sheepishly offered sent a ripple of something heated and primal through her bones. She stopped just short of running a hand over the steamed-over mirror to check her appearance. Who would she find there, behind the mist? Her old self, or whoever this new beast taking her over was?

She smoothed her fingers over the cotton T-shirt and decided not to look. A couple of hurried steps later, she was out the front door, where Kyle immediately jumped out of his chair. The man had good manners, like all army brats.

Or maybe not, she thought a moment later when he was still staring. Maybe she should have used that mirror, after all. "What?"

He jerked his eyes away. "Nothing."

Eyes down, he led the way to the truck and opened the door on her side before circling around to his. It seemed to be jammed, so she stretched across the cab to push it open. By the time she was upright in her own space again, she felt light-headed from the scent of him. A healthy, outdoorsy scent, like wood and fresh air and a homey den, and damned if she didn't lean left to get just a little more.

"A half-hour drive," Kyle said, "Then we meet the pack alpha—the boss." He kept his eyes glued to the road as he drove. "On the ranch."

Ranch? Stef looked left and right. No horses. No cowboys. What ranch?

A ponderous silence filled the cab, a silence that even the vistas of the drive couldn't overcome. She had the urge to fill it with something. Anything. Even awkward conversation would do.

"How long have you lived here?" she started.

"Five, six years."

The army brat in her whistled. "Six years in one place? What does that feel like?"

The creases in his forehead eased just a little bit, but he didn't say what she expected: *Good. It feels good to have a place to call home.*

He just shrugged. "Okay."

"You like it?"

He pursed his lips like he'd never considered the question. "I like it well enough."

She looked out over the landscape. It was dry and harsh, but the open space was intriguing. A place to fill with dreams and hopes, if a person dared.

20

"I was really sorry to hear about your mom," he said in the silence that ensued.

A heavy weight settled in her stomach, like it always did when she thought about her mother. Fifteen was a crappy age to lose your mom, and even a decade passing didn't take away the sorrow.

"How is your mom?" she asked, treading carefully over thin ice.

Now it was his turn to shrug and look into the distance. "She finally split up with Bruce." He shook his head, like he still couldn't understand what drove her to marry his stepfather in the first place. "Married a different guy."

A better guy, she hoped. Though it would be hard to do worse.

"Do you see her much?"

"No," he said, his voice flat and final, and his fingers flexed around the steering wheel. "Do you see much of your dad?"

The lead in her gut settled deeper. "K.I.A." Kyle would know what it meant. *Killed in action;* a nice way to say blown apart by a land mine.

"Jesus, Stef."

She could feel his eyes on her but kept her gaze trained firmly ahead.

"And your brother?" He asked like he was afraid to know.

She shrugged. "He's still in the army." Still trying to follow in their father's footsteps, even if that meant getting killed. Still failing to answer the letters she refused to quit sending because he was all the family she had left.

She made a waving motion with her hands. "Anyway, there it is. Were you ever tempted to enlist?"

He shook his head. "I only ever wanted to be a cop."

She read between the lines. Catch the bad guys. Put them away. Yeah, she could see the logic in that.

The truck crested a hill, and she caught a view into the valley beyond. A splash of irrigated green marked what had to be the ranch: a clutch of low buildings surrounded by a patchwork of paddocks and fields. When Kyle turned off at an unmarked track soon after, she clutched her seat belt. Driving

21

through the desert had a certain suspended-in-time feel to it, but nearing an unknown destination didn't sit well with her nerves. The truck rolled over a low, arching bridge then under a timber gateway where the ranch brand hung: two circles, overlapping by a third. She found herself twisting for a second look as it flashed overhead. Where was he taking her?

"Twin Moon Ranch," Kyle murmured.

When Kyle parked in a central square flanked by century-old cottonwoods, she made no move to get out. She shoved her hands under her thighs, clamping down on herself like someone was about to drag her away. Even when he came around and opened her door, she felt stuck in place. Her chin was nearly touching her chest, her eyes squeezed tight. Maybe she couldn't do this. Maybe she could still find that rattlesnake. Maybe—

"Hey," Kyle whispered.

She tilted her head away.

"They can help."

Her shoulders hunched, a flimsy suit of armor against her fears.

"I can help," he said. "At least, I'll try."

The words warmed up that bleak space between despair and doubt, and she looked up at him. His eyes were steady and promising: Scout's honor. He pulled the door just a little bit wider.

If he'd asked her now, she'd have admitted that the tough guy act was just a show. But he didn't say anything; he just kept promising with those sincere eyes. She took a long, steadying breath, the kind she'd take on the starting line of a road race, then slid out of the car and eyed the building ahead.

The musky scent of wolf greeted her. Something instinctual identified it immediately. Every step felt heavy, every breath forced. The only thing keeping her planting one foot in front of another was Kyle, maintaining an even pace at her side.

Kyle was one thing. But what about the others?

She didn't like this. Didn't like this one bit.

Chapter Five

Kyle tried to convey a sense of confidence as he walked, though he was chastising himself inside. He should have explained about the pack on the drive over: how it worked, what shifters were, where she fit in. But Christ, he barely knew where he fit in.

Fluffy bits of cottonwood tumbled across the open space, and a shadow moved behind one of the council house windows. Was it Ty? Cody? Shit, he really should have given Stefanie a heads up.

"Stef," he started, but it came out too low to be heard over the determined tread of her footsteps. When this woman decided she was ready for something, she was ready. Even if there was no way anyone could be ready for what was sure to come next.

A flicker of a breeze toyed with Stefanie's hair and his gaze couldn't let her go.

Stay removed. Don't get involved. Don't let yourself feel.

His wolf huffed. *Fat chance of that.*

She'd fascinated him from the moment he flipped her over, and now... now *this*. He'd lost a breath or two back home, when she'd come out after her shower. She looked fresher, newer, purer. A little more... alive. She smelled of rosewood and lavender and honeysuckle, and damn it, none of that came from his soap. Her hair was still shining from the shower, and the finger-comb marks begged his hands to plow those furrows for himself. He'd go right from there to the rest of her body, given half a chance. Even if the yellow shirt he'd lent her didn't do much to highlight her figure, he already had a good idea of what was hidden beneath from when he'd pinned her down in the desert. Even now, his heart was skipping at the memory.

The absolutely inappropriate memory. She was the tomboy from next door!

Not any more, she isn't, his wolf rumbled.

Something about seeing her in his shirt was strangely pleasing to his wolf. It was just a plain T-shirt he'd inadvertently shrunk in the wash, but yellow worked on her, calming the effect of her incredible eyes. The brown had always seemed unique: something special inside the ordinary that only found its full voice in her eyes.

Stefanie. She was back in his life. At that moment, he could have caught her and pulled her tight, marveling that one of the few positives in a turbulent life had been allowed to shine back in. She'd always been the funny girl next door, one of the few kids who didn't pry or giggle or tease him into a fight. The only one who knew that when he said no to coming out to play he meant yes, if they'd only asked enough. That his *yes, he was fine,* meant he was anything but. He'd liked her then, and he liked her now, too.

Liked her a little too much for her own good. He stuck his fists into his pockets as he walked and swallowed his wolf's growl of reproach. He'd already let her down. It was his job to take care of her, his job to protect. His job to—

He caught himself there. Since when was any of that his job?

Except, in this case, he felt like he was born for that job.

Damn right, his wolf murmured, studying her every move.

Despite her tough-guy act, he could smell the fear on her, tempered only by exhaustion—and that stiff sense of pride, that dignity. He was leading her into a den of wolves—literally—and yet she was still in control. His own first-days-after were full of fury and violence, when the change was twisting his soul in knots. But maybe that was just him, screwed up as ever on the inside.

There were three steps up to the council house; he remembered it seeming like the long, imposing flight of stairs up the capital building the first time he'd been brought here—brought in by the scruff of his neck, soiled and sour. At least he'd spare Stefanie that indignity. If only he could spare her the rest.

He imagined the discussion that would take place, the hard questions. Even if the pack agreed to shelter her, where would she stay? At Tina's? In the guesthouse? With old Aunt Jean?

With me! Me! His wolf jumped and waved like a kid hoping to be picked for a team.

Keep your distance. Don't get involved.

Right, his wolf snickered. *Try stopping me when I'm already all in.*

Chapter Six

Stef was close to balking and sprinting away when the door swung open and a man with golden blond hair emerged, flashing a smile that could power half of Hollywood.

"Welcome to the ranch!"

She blinked. She'd been expecting more of the dark and silent type, like Kyle. But this man could have been a surfer dude. A model. A champion snowboarder. Anything but a wolf.

Kyle came up alongside her and nodded. "Cody."

When the man came down a step and held a hand out to her, she did her best to deliver a firm shake.

"You must be Stefanie." He grinned like it was the highlight of his day to stop whatever he'd been doing and find out how he could help.

Apparently, Kyle had called ahead. She glanced over, but his gaze was fixed on the dark-haired beauty who appeared in the doorway ahead. Stef's blood surged. The idea of Kyle being friends, neighbors, colleagues, or worse—lovers—with any other woman suddenly grated on her raw nerves. Even her gums ached, especially around her canines.

Which didn't make sense. A guy like Kyle could have any woman he wanted, and that beauty would certainly have her pick of men. So what if the thought sent pinpricks into her heart?

She whipped her face into a neutral expression, determined not to give anything away. It wasn't like she had some kind of claim to Kyle, after all.

A chant started up inside. *Claim,* it said, quiet yet insistent. *Claim.*

She tried not to let envy transfer to her handshake as she approached the woman. "Hi," she said, feeling very much like the country peasant granted an audience with the queen.

"I'm Tina." The woman smiled, and her greeting was gracious, even if she looked weary. Behind the striking looks were carefully schooled features and steely determination. The woman was no pushover, that was for sure. And if she had any claim to Kyle, well, that was no business of Stef's.

So what if the chant was rising up again? *Claim. Claim.*

A tap came on her back; Kyle was nodding her toward the cool shade of the room. In all the uncertainty of the moment, that touch was her anchor. She didn't have to face this storm alone.

A good thing, too, because there was a third introduction to be made, and even Kyle's broad shoulders allowed a deferential tilt to that man.

"This is Ty," Cody said from behind.

The man sat and smoldered, a volcano about to erupt. His piercing gaze fixed on her the way a farmer regards a brewing storm—trouble with a capital T.

The door clicked shut behind her, and a long, silent minute went by. She had the uncomfortable sensation of standing amidst three kings of the food chain, each with his own unassailable power. Ty was the grizzled lion, king of the realm. Cody was a cougar: smooth, silky, and sleek. And Kyle—he was the watchful hawk, circling just out of reach.

The weighty silence made her crave his reassuring touch— and just like that, it was there, a warm hand on her back. Her mind clung to the brief contact and wrapped it like an ember deep inside. She'd take Kyle's softer brand of brooding power over these other forces of nature, any day.

"You found her where?" Ty snapped.

The question was aimed at Kyle as if she was a mongrel found on the side of the road. One with a lot of fleas. She did her best to keep her shoulders back and her chin high, even though what she really wanted was to roll into a tight ball.

"She was up by the mesa."

She watched Kyle's lips shape each letter, his cheeks rise and fall. That face, that voice, were the only familiar things in the room.

"Doing what?"

Kyle hesitated, and the memory of their encounter washed over her like a heat wave. Running and tumbling had somehow turned into touching, sniffing, *wanting—badly*. The chant—*Claim! Claim!*—beat in her mind alongside that memory. It carried her away from this awkward place and into the desert, where the vast openness promised anything was possible. Even escape. She swooped and dove there like an eagle, until a tap broke in to her reverie, snapping her back to the present.

Everyone was looking at her.

"Tell us what happened," Tina said. "Where. When."

Stef stared at the hardwood floor, wishing she could somehow squeeze through the cracks in the floorboards and slither away.

"Last Tuesday," she told the floor. "The seventh. In Colorado."

"Where?" Ty demanded.

"North Ridge."

When the room filled with a hum of recognition, she glanced around, seeing faces of consternation.

"North Ridge," Ty repeated, slowly. His thunderous expression grew darker still.

Kyle exchanged a grim look with Cody.

"You know North Ridge?" she ventured.

Tina answered with a curt nod, and Cody chimed in with an apologetic look. "A wolf pack, not exactly known for their...good manners."

Wolf pack? Her eyes bounced around the room. Is that what this ranch was?

"What the hell were you doing on North Ridge territory?" Ty barked.

She flinched. At her side, something blurred—Kyle, taking a lightning step forward while viciously clearing his throat. Or was that a growl? Ty flushed and she could swear his eyes glowed. They only wavered when a woman's voice sounded from the doorway.

"What my completely insensitive mate is saying," the woman said, "is what business brought you there?"

Stef swiveled and spotted a leggy brunette stalking toward Ty, socking him with a frown.

Mate? The word stuck in her ears.

"Hi, Lana," Cody grinned broadly at the newcomer as Ty lowered his chin.

She got the feeling there weren't too many people who could reprimand Ty. Except maybe this one, his mate. Why not partner or wife? But no, those terms were far too ordinary for the obvious bond between those two. The way Ty's eyes softened when they swung to the woman's protruding baby bump only reinforced the impression.

"Right," he murmured, without the growl this time. "What business brought you there?"

And just like that, all eyes were back on Stef.

"I work for a renewable energy group, advising clients on solar power." Her dream job, it once seemed, giving her the opportunity to travel to interesting places throughout the west while pursuing a career she was passionate about.

Unfortunately, "interesting" places included North Ridge, Colorado.

"I had a bad feeling about the place—and Ron, the ranch manager—right away." She tried to shake the tension away, but all that did was pull her shoulders tighter. She looked at Kyle. Maybe if she pretended he was the only one in the room, she could get the rest out.

You can do it, those blue eyes said. *One word at a time. They can help.*

She doubted anyone could.

I can help.

She took a deep breath and went on.

"I figured Ron was just another eccentric customer looking to live off the grid." He seemed friendly enough, even if he did reek of the hand-rolled cigarettes he smoked. And if he called her back to the ranch again and again before settling on an order, oh well. It was all part of her job.

That's what she thought right up until her fourth trip out to the ranch, when he'd dispensed with pleasantries and broken into a crazy speech about love and mates and forever. His eyes had gleamed with madness as he held her like in a vise-tight grip then bent his head to her neck. Her shouts and kicks pushed him away once, twice—but then he slammed her against a wall and held her tight. And the next thing she knew, there was the cold shock of a bite—the bite of impossibly long teeth sinking into her flesh. She remembered Ron sighing in pleasure, the nauseating tobacco scent, the oozing warmth of her own blood trickling down her neck—

Her hand flew to cover the scar and she broke off, desperately wishing she was someone else, somewhere else. Anywhere but this room full of strangers who were examining her like a new disease. All but Kyle, whose eyes were sorrow and anger and hope, all wrapped up in blue. The golden flakes were back, too. Stefanie blinked, denying her tears a way out, and focused on him until she regained her footing.

"I got away." She rushed through the memories of kicking Ron in the groin, of ramming a palm into his nose to break it. "I got in my car and—"

Ty held up a hand, stopping her flat. "Once?"

Everyone leaned in for her answer.

"How many times did he bite you? Once? Twice?"

"What does it matter?" she snapped. Suddenly, she didn't care if Ty could kill her with a single look. Let him stare her down. If nothing else, it would give her the end she'd so desired.

"It's important," Lana said gently.

Kyle gave her an encouraging nod, and she reluctantly delved back into her memories. She remembered Ron at her throat, not sucking or tearing, just holding. Waiting for something? Or was he just enjoying his sick pleasure? Whatever the case, she had used the lapse to butt her knee into his groin and make her escape.

"Once."

Kyle looked relieved; Ty, unhappy. Cody was unreadable, but Tina and Lana gave her warm looks.

"And then you got away." Tina nodded, her tone telling Stef she did well.

Yes, she had done well. She had gotten away, hadn't she? Still, the thought didn't give her much of a boost.

"Why is one or two bites important?"

"One bite turns, the second bite mates," Tina and Cody said in singsong unison, as if reciting an old saying.

She wasn't sure she wanted to hear more. Turning? Mating? She felt herself leaning in Kyle's direction, seeking out his reassurance.

Lana gave her a slow look-over then turned to Kyle. "You mean you haven't told her?"

She snapped to attention as he gave a sheepish shake of the head. "Tell me what?"

Silence all around.

"Tell me what?"

Chapter Seven

Everyone looked at the floor, at each other, at the walls. Anywhere but at her. Even Ty had his eyes on his mate until Tina picked up where she left off.

"He didn't tell you who we are. What we are. What you are becoming." She said it gently, as if speaking to a frightened child.

Stef closed her eyes, but even that didn't stop the images Tina's words conjured: Ron, with his protruding fangs. Her dreams, filled with howls and hunger. Kyle, with his claw-mark scars. The old woman at the trading post.

"Skinwalker," she whispered, forcing her eyes open.

Tina rewarded her with a sympathetic smile. "Shifter."

She wobbled slightly. "Werewolf?"

"Humans use that word," Tina said, "but it comes with so many myths; we prefer shifter."

Right, myths. Werewolf myths. And then there was that part about humans. Like there was an us and a them.

Kyle, she noticed, started rubbing his scarred shoulder.

One bite turns... She touched her neck gingerly. The gash Ron had ripped into her throat had healed far too quickly to be normal.

"So I'll turn into..." She wasn't sure how to finish that sentence. "Into..." She broke off again, backing toward the door. Her eyes darted around the room then locked in on Kyle's. There—the next best thing to running outside and gulping fresh air: looking into those baby blues.

They can help. I can help.

She concentrated there, watching the gold flicker like so many fireflies as she tried to regain her control. "Turn. Change. How?" she demanded.

"The first bite turns," Tina explained as calmly as if she were pouring tea at a ladies' luncheon. "The second bite mates."

"Mates." She parried the verb away, unwilling to accept it.

"Wolves don't marry. We mate. For life."

Okay, that part didn't sound as twisted as the rest. Until Tina dropped the other shoe, that is.

"Wolves don't bite humans just to turn them. This Ron wanted you as his mate."

Stef pretended to keep her composure despite the ice sliding down her spine. "Well, too bad for him."

But Tina was shaking her head sadly. "Wolves don't give up when it comes to mates."

She saw Ty's eyes flick to Lana's and fill with a fiery vow that promised death and destruction to anyone who tried to part them. Cody's eyes were focused somewhere far out a window on the south side, while Tina seemed wistful.

Kyle, on the other hand, looked straight at her with golden fireworks shooting around his eyes.

She shook herself a little. Yes, she could believe in a special link between mates. Which was fine for two people who wanted each other—but she didn't want anything to do with Ron.

"I won't go with him," she said so loudly, it was nearly a shout.

"It's not that simple," Cody said. "Technically, that bite puts you in his pack."

She gaped. "The North Ridge pack?"

Tina nodded, looking grim. Clearly, they weren't telling her everything about their Colorado brethren.

"I won't go."

"You belong to them," Tina said.

Kyle slid close enough that she could feel his body heat, but even that didn't help.

"I belong?" She was shouting now. What the hell was this? "I belong to no one. No pack."

Ty put up a hand, and everyone went still. "Listen, we'll do what we can. But this is the way it is. His bite marked you as a member of his pack, and every wolf needs a pack."

Everyone in the room nodded except for her and Kyle. "I don't need a pack! I don't want a pack!"

The outburst only earned her looks of sympathy or disbelief.

"The need will start to pull you in after your first couple of changes," Tina said. "Besides, a lone female wolf is an easy target. If you don't belong to a pack, any male can claim you with a bite. That's the second bite. Unclaimed females who belong to a pack are usually left alone, but lone wolves..." She trailed off, shaking her head.

Stef paled, picturing Ron. What kind of crazy medieval world had she just stepped into? And where the hell was the way out?

Ty and Cody were exchanging looks the way other people exchanged words, only no sound came out. Then Ty gave a curt nod and addressed everyone in the room—everyone but her. "Right now, we have to decide where to keep her."

"Keep me?" Her face went hot.

"Safe," Lana rushed to add, shooting Ty another look.

"Keep you safe," Kyle echoed, his eyes shining.

She'd never feel safe among these people—these wolves. Her throat tightened as her hands twisted the fabric of her shirt.

"Why don't you show Stefanie around, Kyle?" Cody said, his voice like bottled calm, uncorked just for this occasion. "We can meet again after lunch."

She race-walked to the door and shot out into daylight with Kyle half a step behind and let the sun fill her with the warmth that had seeped away with every terrifying word. Words like shifter, werewolf, and mate. She paced away from the building, away from the central square, seeking the open desert and some sense of calm.

Kyle stayed with her, silent and steady as a faithful dog, letting her determine the way. She found a dirt track and made for the top of a ridge where she sucked in the views and told herself not to run.

Yet.

Chapter Eight

"So what happens now?" she blurted. "I grow fangs and fur? I howl at the moon?"

Silence answered—that vast, squeezing silence of the desert, where only the wind whispered through the brush. She would have screamed in frustration if Kyle hadn't finally murmured a reply.

"We don't howl at the moon."

We? She wasn't sure she wanted to be included in that club.

From the corner of her eye, she saw him run an uncertain hand through his hair, making the short ends spike even more.

"We howl to... get things out."

"Like what?"

Kyle kicked a rock into the undergrowth then shrugged. "Things you can't put in words."

She was about to shout something about having a lot of words to speak right now—four-letter words—until she saw his face. Drawn and dark, he stood staring at something in his past. What things did Kyle have to say that couldn't be put into words? Did it have to do with the fact that he lived alone, so far from the rest? If wolves were social creatures who needed a pack, what kept him apart? Kyle had always kept to himself, though, even as a kid. Why?

A thousand questions she couldn't ask. Maybe she should try howling them to the moon sometime.

So not funny, said that inner voice that seemed to get louder with each passing hour. She set off walking again, going somewhere—anywhere. Kyle stayed three steps behind, brooding but silent.

In any other situation, she would have reveled in the long, open vistas, the undulating terrain that hinted at a thousand corners to explore. But her eyes were as unsettled as her soul, darting suspiciously about, examining the ranch for any outward sign of its secret.

"It looks so...normal."

"It is normal," he insisted. "Kind of."

Which just about summed it up. On the surface, it looked all the world like any other rural community. An inner ring of tidy homes with flower pots and hummingbird feeders formed the heart of the ranch. Beyond that cluster, an outer circle of fenced-in fields dotted with livestock gradually gave way to open desert.

"It's a good place, Stef. Good people."

"It's not much different than North Ridge."

His voice went growly at that. "This is nothing like North Ridge."

The truth was, the vibe was totally different. Maybe it really was as nice as he said. But werewolves? Who was she trying to kid?

She stalked past a barn that had been converted into a community hall where a wall fluttered with flyers that announced ordinary community events: barbecues, soccer games, reading clubs. Someone somewhere was practicing the piano, and there was even a one-room schoolhouse and a playground full of energetic kids.

"Hey, Miss Luth!" The voice of one of the children carried as they walked past. "What do you call an alligator in a vest?"

"What, Timmy?" The teacher sounded like she had all the patience in the world.

"An investigator!"

Stef walked on. It was all perfectly normal—except for one thing. They were all wolves. At any point of day or night these people—these shifters—could twist their bodies into wolf form and tear off into the hills. Voluntarily, according to Kyle, though she couldn't see the appeal. Apparently, their Navajo neighbors were a pack, too—a pack of coyote shifters.

Right, coyote shifters. She had just nodded at that point. Nothing could surprise her any more.

Or so she thought. Because when Kyle led her to lunch in an oak-beamed dining hall where pack members shared meals several times a week, she balked. The sight of all those people— kids, families, elders—all of them werewolves? It looked like a scene out of a Norman Rockwell painting, and that's what tipped her over the edge. There was no way to tell shifters from humans. The harmony of the scene seemed a lie; any minute now, the fangs would come out and the feeding frenzy would begin.

Her knees locked as she stood frozen on the threshold.

I can't do this. Can't. Won't. Don't want any part of this.

If she could have screamed and run there and then, she would have. But her legs wouldn't heed the command and neither did her voice. She stood trembling in the doorway, breaking out in a sweat.

Kyle turned, crooking his head in a gesture so like the old days that it stopped her just short of a full-on meltdown.

"You okay?"

"Fine," she whispered and promptly spun on her heel. She speed-walked away with vision blurred by tears and all but shouldered Tina aside. "Sorry," she blurted, hurrying on.

She only stopped when the notes of the piano reached her again in the shade of a barn. She leaned her forehead against the weathered planking, palms flat against the coarse wood, fighting back a bubble of hysteria.

Fine. I'm fine. All fine...

That there were wolves all around her wasn't the only problem. The fact that she was turning into one... Her fingernails scratched at the wood, fighting the thought away. The deep breaths she tried weren't working; they were too shallow, too forced, like she was running for her life and not hiding behind a barn.

Like at the start of a race. Breathe. Stay in control.

Right, control. She'd never been less in control. And the rare times in her life when she thought she had been, those were a mirage. The constant moves as a child, the awful series of losses she'd endured. And now this—getting ripped out of the life she'd forged for herself and being thrown straight to the wolves. Literally.

The scuff of footsteps sent her heart hammering, her body closer to the wall. Let whomever it was think she was mentally unstable. It wasn't far from the truth.

As the steps drew nearer, a scent reached her, and her knees wobbled. It was Kyle. Kyle Williams, back in her life.

That part. . . She sucked in a long breath, feeling her nerves gradually settle. That part, she liked. Why, she wasn't in the mood to examine. Only that she felt the rightness of it from the root of her soul. Wolf or human, it didn't matter with him. She let her eyes crack open and peeked, trying to drink in the steadiness he emanated.

"Hey," he started in a voice much softer than his protective stance.

She gulped back the knot in her throat and tried shaking away the tears of relief. It was one thing to be a mess inside; it was different to let Kyle see.

She wished it was him she could cling to instead of the weathered wall. He'd be as big and solid and strong as the barn, that was for sure. But she'd never been one to throw herself at a man, and never wanted to be.

Except this wasn't just any man. It was the boy next door, and she knew his secrets. Some of them, anyway. Couldn't she share a few of her own?

He stepped closer, an inch away, and the warm tickle of breath at her ear brought her the safe sense of an army at her back. An army of one, who'd never ever failed her, and never ever would.

"Hey," Kyle tried again, and his voice was so gentle, it might have been a dream. His hand warmed her shoulder, the touch light but steady.

She angled her head, trapped between the urge to give in and the all-too-practiced habit of hiding away. Kyle had his share of worries; he didn't need hers.

"Stef," he said, his voice husky. It wasn't pity, though. It was a plea.

A ripple of shame went through her. She'd hurt him by rushing away from the dining room. Worried him, too, judging by the waver in his voice. Couldn't she spare a thought for anyone but herself? Kyle had come out of nowhere to help and brought her to his pack, and she'd been less than gracious in return. Turned her tail and run—even from him.

Never from him! cried an inner voice, deep and defiant.

She wasn't good at comforting herself, but she could comfort him. She turned, intending to say it out loud. *I'm sorry. I'm fine. Everything will be okay.* But the moment she saw his face, she knew she couldn't lie. Not to him. She stood there hopelessly, watching the gold sparks in his eyes.

They both started an inhale at the exact same moment, and before she even got to the exhale, Kyle pulled her into a hug that fit like a second skin. She buried her face in his shoulder and let herself pretend it was he who needed the holding, not her.

He smelled so good: of dry, open spaces with a hint of pine. No—oak, the kind you'd make a shield of, solid and stubborn and pure of heart. There was even a perfect grip where the muscles of his shoulders met the tight cords of his waist. The knots of her own body started to unwind, one after another, as if they hadn't been tied at all, just bundled up and waiting for his magic touch.

"Stef," he whispered. "It'll be all right."

When he said it, she could believe it.

A hum started up in her ears, just as it had when he'd first caught her on the mesa and pinned her down. A hum that called for closer and more, so insistent that she had to obey. Kyle must have heard it, too, because his hands ran along her sides, then traced some secret message on her spine. She nestled closer, her nose followed the line of his neck.

"Kyle. . ."

When she turned her face, his was already there, as if they were playing out a scene they'd lived in a previous life. She caught a glimpse of gold flickering in his eyes before she closed her own, because the cushion of his lips against hers was already enough to push her dangerously close to the edge. Soft and dry, they set off a melting sensation deep inside. His fingers in her hair were a safety net closing softly around her, promising everything would be all right.

A backlog of grateful words built in her throat, but all that came out was a muffled whimper as she worked her lips against his. An open O, a mumble of an M, then a long lick of an L. She leaned back until she had the wall of the barn on one side and the wall of Kyle on the other. Heaven was the slot between those walls. Heaven was the heat of his body, the twitch in his jaw that begged for more.

Heaven was Arizona, with Kyle.

All the times they'd never kissed—never even thought of kissing—ran through her mind, starting with the shed in the back of the school grounds when she was twelve, all the way up to the drive to the ranch in his truck. How could she have missed those chances? Everything she'd been searching for in her life was in that kiss. Her heart was pounding half out of her chest, her hands tight on his shirt. That kiss was the only good thing that had happened to her in the past week. The best thing that had happened to her in a long, long time.

If her lips hadn't been busy with his, she'd have cooed in delight.

Her hands were just sliding toward the curve of his ass, his fingers just finding the swell of her breasts, when the hum crackled. Kyle broke away with a faint gasp half a second before a shadow stepped around the corner.

"Lunchtime!"

It was Cody, cheery as a schoolboy on a Friday afternoon.

She whirled, letting go of Kyle's hand in a motion akin to ripping a bandage from a raw wound. A wail went through her body even as her hands hurried to straighten her shirt.

Stef blinked. Where did the hum go?

"Cody..." Kyle growled.

Where was the certainty she'd felt only seconds before? Jesus, what had she done?

"Hungry?" Cody beckoned with a hand.

She ran a hand over her cheek, already feeling it flush, and wished she could melt right into the wall. Maybe if she became another shadow in that weathered surface, everyone would leave her alone. Everyone but Kyle.

"Everything all right?"

That was Tina, pushing past Cody. Her earth-black eyes tracked over Stefanie's face, then over to Kyle, and finally narrowed on Cody.

"Men can be such idiots," she sniffed, addressing no one in particular before pointing an accusing finger at Cody and Kyle in turn. "The last thing she needs is a dining room full of shifters."

Stef's mouth moved, wanting to jump to Kyle's defense. But Tina was already leading her away with a gentle kind of insistence that didn't broker a no.

"Come with me. We'll have a nice, quiet lunch in a nice, quiet place."

Stef glanced back and faltered. Kyle was so big, so sure, so. . . so unassailable, and yet there he was, looking as droopy and distraught as a chastised puppy. She wanted to rush back and tell him it was okay, everything was okay—just like she'd wanted to so many times in the past. But right now, those words—*it's okay, everything is okay*—were coming from Tina, and Stef didn't have a chance to pull away.

Chapter Nine

Tina led Stefanie down a meandering path in the shade of the cottonwoods to a tidy adobe bungalow with a lush green lawn. The place screamed *structure* and *order* from every manicured flower bed to every white-trimmed window.

"This is my place. Come on in."

The inside was as neat as the outside: a study in single female habitation. Every cushy throw pillow, every diamond-patterned rug was perfect, yet something about the place wept. Stef found herself studying Tina as she bustled around a kitchen decorated with needlepoint designs with yearning messages like *Home Sweet Home.*

"It's very nice," Stef said. "Have you seen Kyle's place?"

She didn't mean it as a test, but it sure wouldn't hurt to know how intimate Tina was with Kyle's home.

Then again, maybe it would hurt. Bad.

But Tina just laughed, and the envy sloughed away. "No, but I can imagine it. Chaos."

"Chaos is close," she smiled. "Oh, sorry. Can I help with lunch?"

"I've got it. You relax."

Right, relax. The word was like a cue to let the tension roll back in. So Stef wandered a little, finding a thousand cryptic clues to her host's existence in the room. The neatly stacked magazines, the self-help books. The refrigerator covered with photos and newspaper clippings.

She leaned in for a closer look. The clippings all came out of the sports pages: a season schedule for the San Diego Padres, a report on spring training. She looked at Tina then back at the clippings. "You like baseball?"

"No, not really," Tina hummed absent-mindedly while washing lettuce at the sink.

Stef squinted at the other clippings. One player was setting new batting records, while another had been injured, it seemed. No, wait, the same player. She glanced at Tina. What was that all about?

But she had enough of her own mysteries to sort out, so she let her eyes wander over the photos instead. Her first reaction was relief: not one showed Tina in a tight embrace with Kyle. Actually, there wasn't a single photo of Kyle. Most of the photos were of children. There was Cody, snuggling a pink-faced baby bundled in a pink blanket with a big black dog leaning over his shoulder for a peek. There was a striking, dark-haired man steadying a toddler with one massive hand. He looked all the world like Ty, except this version wore a soft expression and a fascinated smile. Farther along the same cluttered collage were shots of Tina holding the same youngsters in various poses, so close and so tight that Stef could feel the ache.

"That's my niece, Tana," Tina said over her shoulder, and Stef nearly jumped. The woman moved with the stealth of a cat.

"And my brother Cody's daughters." Her finger tapped the pictures.

Blond, sunny Cody, related to this dark raven? "He's your brother?"

Tina laughed like it was an old joke. "Well, my half brother. Ty's the oldest, and then me. Then Cody and Carly came along."

Tina must have sensed Stef scraping her memory for faces that might be a sister to Cody, because she shook her head. "Carly lives in California with her mother."

Tina tapped another picture, and another. Her finger wavered a moment over another image of the baseball player then skipped right over to the next one. "That's my aunt Jean..."

Stef held her tongue. Any questions she asked would give Tina free rein to ask right back, and she wasn't in the mood for another interrogation. Not unless it came from a tall, dark cop with short, spiky hair.

Tina motioned toward the table, piled with a mountain of food. "Eat. You look like a scarecrow."

Stef squeezed her hands against her shirt in silent protest. This yellow T-shirt suited her just fine. Then her fingers found her waistband. Okay, maybe her shorts were a bit loose. As in, hanging off her hips. And yeah, there might have been a bit more rib showing than usual. The past couple of days had been filled with more running than eating—and not the kind of running that filled her with weary satisfaction.

While she dug in to lunch with a ravenous hunger that swept over her like a burst dam, Tina started an ode to the ranch and the seasons and the beauty of the desert. Her voice was just lulling Stef into thinking Twin Moon was paradise when a cat moved outside the window. It sat in the sun, casually cleaning itself by licking a paw then scrubbing its ears. Stef wondered if the cat could shift forms. A werecat?

She wouldn't be surprised.

Nor was she surprised when Tina made a smooth segue into the ugly details of werewolfdom. When the subject turned to topics like shifting, pack structure, and mating, Stef put her fork down and twisted her hands under the table. No longer hungry, she eyed the door.

Escape. Her mind was crying for it. Soon, she feared, she'd be screaming it out loud.

The warnings uttered in the council house came back to her in a rush. She belonged to North Ridge. She belonged to Ron.

The need will start to pull you in after your first couple of changes, Tina had said.

So how the hell do I keep him away?

She must have said it out loud because Tina answered. "We'll think of something."

Somehow, though, Tina didn't sound so sure.

Maybe she could go to Oregon, where her mother's relatives lived. Or Georgia, where her dad's closest friends were. They were all tough army guys, so maybe...

But Tina shook her head sadly, like she'd been reading Stef's mind. "A lone female wolf is an easy target."

47

"But what about you?" Stef blurted. "You're single, right?"

The light in Tina's eyes faded, and her cheeks tightened just a pinch. "It's hard not to be single when your father is—or was—the pack alpha and your brothers are ready to kick the ass of any man they don't approve of right over the state line. All in the name of protecting my virtue, of course." She said it lightly, but there was bitterness between the words.

Still, Stef couldn't help sounding wistful. "Sounds good." She'd had a loving dad and a protective older brother, once upon a time.

Tina just sighed. "Believe me, it has its disadvantages."

Stef looked around the perfect, empty house and gave a little nod. "I guess it would."

Tina studied her over her glass of juice and shook her head a little bit. "We'll think of something. Somehow."

Only *something* and *somehow* weren't much of a comfort. Not right now.

Things were no different that night when Stef lay curled in a tight ball in bed in a small building Tina called the guest adobe. Another crazy concept, because what kind of guests would a ranch run by werewolves get? Vampires, maybe? Shapeshifting bears?

Or maybe just other wolves. Like herself.

She pulled the sheet from chin level to over her head, pretending she could escape her doubts. She'd been so naive in Colorado. Was she being too trusting now?

A wolf pack, not exactly known for good manners.

Technically, you belong to North Ridge.

What if all this was a ruse? Maybe these wolves were doing nothing more than keeping her busy until Ron could show up and claim his mate.

Images assaulted her mind: visions of her visits to a ranch much like this, where a beast disguised as a man sprouted fangs and forced her against a wall, then leaned in and bit deep. She remembered the struggle, the man's crazed eyes. His shout of pain as she lashed out. No matter how tightly she clutched the sheets or squeezed her eyelids together, the images wouldn't go away.

And it was only getting worse. The images were sharper and more urgent, hinting at something worse to come. Like Ron, coming to get her. Ron, pinning her against another wall. If he trapped her again, would she have the strength to resist?

The need will start to pull you in.

If Ron came for her, no one would care. No one would come to help her.

Kyle would come, that inner voice said, so firm and sure that her heart beat faster.

But then the moon came out, nearly full, and her blood tingled the way it had right after the bite. As if Ron were calling to her from wherever he was, assuring her he was on his way.

Mate, he said, his lips pulling back in greed.

Mine, he insisted, leaning in close.

She let out a strangled cry and jerked right out of bed, poised to ward off her attacker. But she was alone, the night-time silence broken only by the desperate gulping of her breath. She sank to the mattress a moment later, head in her trembling hands, and wondered what she'd lose first: her mind, her body, or her soul?

Chapter Ten

Don't worry. The ranch is safe.
Chill out. She'll be fine.

Kyle slammed a fist into the uneven wallboards of the old bunkhouse on the outskirts of the ranch, replaying Cody's casual words. Like he could just go home and call it a night. Turn his back and walk away.

The thing was, he'd done that a thousand times on the job. So what was so different this time?

It's completely different, his wolf snarled.

This wasn't a job. This was Stef.

It was bad enough he'd screwed everything up by bringing her to the dining hall then caught her off guard with that stolen kiss. There was no way he could just drive away after what that kiss did to him.

It had taken everything he had to give her some space that afternoon. That evening, too, while his wolf paced his insides to bits. Now, he was supposed to be settling in for the night in the old bunkhouse. Instead, he was tearing down the walls.

Chill out? Don't worry?

Easy for Cody to say. He wasn't the one with a...a... Kyle struggled to finish his own thought. How would he fill in that blank? A friend whose life was on the line?

Friend? His wolf grunted. *What kind of pansy-ass word is that?*

He pulled his fist back from the splintered hole he had just made, and a breath of night air filtered in, carrying the truth. Stefanie wasn't just a friend. She'd always been more than that, and the grown-up version of the spunky adolescent stirred things in him that he could never associate with just a friend.

51

The way he'd lost himself in her scent and in her kiss told him she was more than that. Much more.

Try mate.

And right on cue, it all came back: the flavor of her kiss, the texture of her skin. The trust in her eyes, giving his wolf all kinds of bad ideas—and his human side, too. He was breathing far too quickly just at the memory of it. He'd never had a kiss like that.

Mate. Mine!

Maybe the tingling had nothing to do with her being a Changeling, and everything to do with being his destined mate.

Destined mates were rare occurrences; the realization should have been a cause for celebration. But if Stef was his mate, destiny had a twisted sense of humor. She'd been brutally claimed by a rival male, and fighting for her would mean dragging his whole pack into trouble—maybe even war.

Christ, could she really be his destined mate?

No, it had to be the Changeling in her, right?

He kicked the door open and stalked out into the night. Maybe a run would help. Taking a deep breath, he shifted, letting the wolf out at last. And thank God for that, because things seemed clearer when he was in canine form. Simpler. There was duty and honor and the pull of the moon and not much else. He could run and howl and let his soul out of its dungeon for just a little while.

Except tonight, there was more to it than that. There was a tickling, insistent feeling. A hunger. What was that all about?

Try love. His wolf grinned, leaping over a ditch.

Love, or greed?

Love, the wolf insisted, and then chuckled. *Maybe with just a little greed.*

Whatever it was, the emotion came paired with hate—that burning, foul taste that came when he pictured the scar on Stef's neck. If only shifters could jump time the way they jumped between two bodies; he'd go back a week and stop her from stepping foot on North Ridge territory in the first place. What had she been thinking, going there alone? He wanted to ferret out her boss, rip him limb from limb then throw the pieces into the same gully where he'd stash the gutted remains of Ron, once he got his claws on that son of a bitch.

First Ron, then the boss, his wolf corrected.

That's when he knew he was in trouble. Because when his human side let the wolf become the strategist, well...

I got this, man. Trust me.

That might have been comforting, except for the fact that you could never trust your inner wolf. That was the first thing he'd decided when he'd been turned. Wolves were all about impulse and instinct, not reason or logic, and only the latter would save Stef.

Wanna bet? his wolf muttered back.

He took off on a wide arc around the ranch, padding fast and furious over rough terrain. Up past the creek and the fork in the trail marked by a bull's skull, then higher still to a ridge where he paused. Sat. Studied. Below, the lights of the ranch shone yellow in the inky night. It was quiet; everyone was tucked into their homes and settling in for family time.

The old stab of envy hit him, and his wolf parked his rump on the cool ground, lifted his muzzle, and howled. Long and low and warbling, wishing his wasn't the only voice filling the desert air that night. He could hear the empty echo of his own howl stretch into the hills then fade into darkness.

Behind the eastern hills, he could feel the pulse of the moon, taunting him. Soon, it would rise over the horizon, plump but for a sliver at one edge.

Tomorrow, most of the pack would be out to revel in the moonlight, but tonight it was just him. He gulped then and stopped singing, listening to the desert slumbering. The quiet could mean anything: just another peaceful night, or danger in the shadows.

He gave his wolf coat an unhappy shake and took off again.

Chill out. She'll be fine.

How could Stefanie be fine if some bastard of a shifter was after her? How could she be fine without someone to protect her?

He completed a full loop, always testing, searching, alert for anything out of the ordinary. Catching the recent scent of

Zack and Rae bolstered him a little. The pack's best eyes and ears were on duty that night. Not that he could relax, but he could leave the outer perimeter to them. He needed to be closer.

Closer.

Very close.

He circled the ranch, spiraling in endless laps until his paws were trampling a path around a single building: the guesthouse. He could scent his brown-eyed girl inside—the pure, uncomplicated soul that was Stefanie. The smell of all-consuming fear came through the walls, and it killed him to know she was afraid. If he could, he'd slip inside and turn a few circles around her body, too. But she'd hardly be comforted by a wolf crashing through her door, so he settled for circling the house again and again.

He lost count of laps by the time two wolves trotted past, and though Kyle knew perfectly well they were packmates and not intruders, he couldn't hold back a growl. A don't-fuck-with-my-foul-mood growl that carried over the deserted lane.

One of the wolves was sunny blond, the other the color of champagne. Cody and Heather, their fur thick with the musk of sex. And why not? They'd put in a long day's work and earned their reward: a little downtime together. Nothing wrong with a little fun.

Except fun didn't fit into Kyle's world right now. Not with Stef in danger. Not with everything out of balance.

He snorted at himself. Who was he kidding? There hadn't been fun or balance in his life since... since... His mind went into rewind, searching his memories until he came up blank.

When Cody shook his fur and approached, the fur on Kyle's back spiked into a razor's edge.

Didn't I tell you to go home?

Kyle bared his teeth in response and let a growl build in the back of his throat. The empty house on the edge of the ranch wasn't home. Wherever Stef was, that was home.

I dare you to take another step, his growl conveyed.

Cody halted in his tracks and cocked his head. It wasn't often that the pack's co-alpha got ordered around. Not by anyone but his brother, at least.

Cody stretched his muzzle out toward Kyle. *Hey, man, I told you not to worry about—*

Kyle snapped at him. If he wanted to worry, he damn well would.

That was his wolf half, at least. The human part buried deep inside watched in shock as his jaws clicked together an inch in front of the co-alpha's nose.

There was a moment of surprised silence before Cody started rumbling, too, taking up a fighting stance.

Watch it, Kyle.

You watch it.

You—

A high-pitched whine broke in to their snarling match as Heather stepped between them and nudged Cody back a step. *Um, guys?*

Kyle gave himself a rough shake. Jesus, he'd just snapped at one of the pack's two leaders—and the closest thing he had to a friend. What the hell was he thinking? It wasn't Cody he wanted to tear to pieces, it was Ron.

But he'd be damned if he let anyone—anyone!—close to the guesthouse tonight.

I told you she'd be fine, Cody's voice sounded in his mind. It was gritty, like voices always were when they communicated in wolf form.

I told you I wasn't leaving, he spit back.

Then Heather chimed in again—*Boys, boys. Enough already!*—and Cody sighed. He turned to Heather and rubbed his muzzle along her neck. Then the two of them turned and walked away, their sides brushing.

Be my guest. Cody's tail flicked as he went. *Stand guard all night.*

Exactly what Kyle intended to do.

He could hear Heather pushing her thoughts to Cody, forcefully enough that he could hear her, too.

I remember someone standing guard outside my house all night, she said, a little tease in her voice.

That was different, Cody answered, letting Kyle in on every word.

Heather just laughed. *Wanna bet?*

Cody pulled up short and swung his head between Kyle and the guesthouse until a soft kind of realization washed over his eyes. He blinked a few times then shook his ruff. *Jesus, man. I hope you know what you're doing.*

Kyle kept his answer to himself. *Christ, I hope so, too.*

He watched them go, that perfectly matched pair. Heather wound herself along Cody's side then dipped under his neck in a wolf sign of approval. The two trotted off, and the image stuck in Kyle's mind. Of being rubbed that way—by Stef. Of trotting into the night, side by side. That easy acceptance, that instant understanding. That sense of belonging.

His wolf gave a hollow huff then turned back to the bungalow and began circling it again. Dreaming wouldn't get him anywhere. He'd tried dreaming himself into a different life as a kid, and all that accomplished was proving how futile hope was. His job was to protect, to prevent evil. Now more than ever—because this wasn't just anyone. It was Stef.

And this wasn't just any night. The more he walked, the more he sensed it in the air. Something faint and thin, but definitely there. Something evil, like a poisonous fog.

A moment later he was snarling in recognition. It was Ron, seeking Stefanie out from a distance. Trying to hone in on her, itching for that second bite.

Come to me, mate, came the whisper in the night.

Kyle pointed his nose north and growled. He made another round of the old adobe, slower now. He was no magician, but damn it, he would keep her safe. Every step became a deliberate act as he concentrated on erecting a wall of sheer stubborn willpower around Stefanie. A bristling wall that would make that coward Ron run for his life.

He rumbled as he walked, rubbing his musk on every wall and every bush. He'd mask her scent with his own and secret her away. His mind cast up battlements, watchtowers, and catapults, all of them howling the same message: *There is nothing for you here.* He imagined the defenses going up, brick by brick, as if they were a physical thing instead of ephemeral, and power flowed from him as from a tap. Let Ron seek. He'd find more than he bargained for.

Adrenaline coursed through his veins like the soldier's high he'd heard about—the one that could fuel a man for hours if his cause was just. Around and around, losing track of time and place, pouring everything he had into protecting Stef.

He was stepping into yet another lap when the moon, already long past its zenith, whispered, *Enough.* He paced one more lap around the old adobe, assuring himself that that probing outside force had given up, at least for the night. Then he hauled himself up on the porch, turned three circles, and slumped down in front of the door, utterly drained. With a heavy sigh, he tucked his nose under his tail, and closed his eyes in an approximation of sleep. But his ears stuck up like a couple of rotating radar domes, fully alert.

Stef Alt, back in his life. He'd be damned if he ever let her go.

Chapter Eleven

Pink morning light filled the room with a cheery glow. Stef could sense it, even from under the sheets. Everything was peaceful. The only reminder of her torturous night was the bedding—damp and twisted from sweat and fear. But that had only lasted the first part of the night. Eventually, the fear had ebbed away, and the house that had first felt like a cage became a safe haven where she could finally drift off to sleep.

She was still half asleep, lingering in her last dream. One in which she'd been intimately wrapped around a man. A good man, not a monster. If she kept her eyes closed, she could still imagine Kyle spooned along her body.

Of course, it was just a dream, but one worth hanging on to—even rewinding and reliving a couple of dozen times.

It started the same way every time: he would appear like a spark of light in the otherwise bleak world of her imagination and pull her close, just like he'd done at the barn.

"Stef," he'd whisper, and she'd whisper right back.

"Kyle."

Like he was hers, and she was his, and both of them knew it.

His touch was warm and tender and incredibly right, and she shaped her body to his like they were practiced lovers. Then she touched every inch of him, from the bulk of his shoulders to the smooth of his chest. His hands slid over her, too, and everything she'd been ready to give up on came giggling back to life. Her face went warm, her core even warmer, and when his hands palmed her breasts, it was like she'd immersed herself in a hot bath. Make that a hot tub, with the jets aimed at all the right places.

Her chuckle climbed to the rafters. Kyle was about the last person she could imagine in a hot tub. She'd only ever been in one once, but hey, this was her dream and she was running with it. She imagined sliding a hand underwater and working the length of him until he was hard and high and whispering her name like no man had ever done before. Looking at her through half-lidded eyes that said she was a thing of wonder and not the skinny kid from next door. She'd pull him closer than close, wrap her legs around his waist and urge him inside.

Then he'd work them both into a raging heat that threatened to consume the night, and she'd rock with him, clutching with her inner muscles to push him over the edge half a second before she took off, too. Flying, flying, diving through the night.

"Kyle."

She sighed out loud, holding on to the warm glow. A dream shouldn't be the best sex she'd ever had, but it was. They did it again and again, and each time, he took her breath away.

Kyle. A lover, not just a friend.

The feeling lasted even after she showered, dressed, and tentatively pulled the front door open. She breathed deeply, and there it was: a promise, hanging in the air. A promise that somehow, everything would be all right. She found herself sinking down on the mat in front of the door. The spot seemed ridiculously cozy, perfect for hugging her knees and soaking in the sun.

She was just drifting off into another sizzling dream when Tina came up and shattered the bubble.

"Morning!"

"Morning," Stef mumbled, wishing it was Kyle there. Where was he anyway? What fantasies were playing in his mind?

"How about breakfast?" Tina offered, leading her away.

She reluctantly shook off the fantasy. At least her blissful morning made up for a miserable night.

There were an awful lot of paw prints around the bungalow, she noticed. They formed a track, like the kind left behind by an old-fashioned pony ride that went around and around.

Which didn't bother her in itself—in fact, something about it set off an inner glow. But the track was like a moat, and the minute she crossed it, the world came crashing back in.

Wolves. Shifters. Mates. A world she wanted no part of.

"So, I wanted to show you the paddocks..."

Tina was either oblivious or pretending to be because she took off on a post-breakfast tour to every corner of the ranch, from the barns to the irrigation channels and the schoolhouse. Stef dragged her heels the whole time. She didn't want views or facts or introductions. She wanted...Kyle.

His name popped right into her mind. He hadn't left, had he? The thought had her nostrils flaring, desperate to locate him. And they did—he was out there somewhere, not far away.

For a warm instant, she felt better, but then it hit her. Jesus, it was really happening. She was turning into a wolf, sniffing the air. Soon she'd be down on all fours, scratching an ear with her back foot and peeing on bushes to mark her turf. A line of sweat broke out along her forehead as she fisted her hands in her shirt.

His shirt.

She pulled the collar up to her nose and took a deep breath of it.

"How are you doing?" Tina asked.

"Fine," she blurted, pretending to study the greenhouse. The one around the back, full of rich colors that contrasted with the dustier desert hues. But there was beauty in the open landscape, too. Just a subtler one. The desert was like Kyle: bristly and rough on the outside, contemplative and quiet inside. Full of hidden secrets, like the wrinkles in the hills.

"And over here we have the pump house..."

She made it through an endless morning and through another lunch, this time with Tina and two nice old ladies named Jean and Ruth. Stef just couldn't picture them changing into anything but...well, nice old ladies.

"So lovely that you've dropped in on us," Jean gushed, as if she really had dropped in and not been blown in by some twist of fate.

Fate brought us to him, said a faint, scratchy voice from somewhere inside.

She looked out the window and tapped her foot against the floor. Where was he?

"And how long will you stay with us?" Ruth asked, her face bright.

Stef looked at Tina, and Tina looked at the floor.

"Um...I'm not quite sure."

The old ladies didn't miss a beat. "And you're an old friend of Kyle's! Isn't that sweet."

Sweet, like his kiss. Like his soft touch on her back when she needed it most. Like the little warble in his voice when he said her name.

"Such a nice young man," Ruth nodded.

"Reminds me of that Baker boy, don't you agree, Ruth?" Jean winked.

Tina cleared her throat sharply, and they went back to stirring their tea.

Yes, they really were nice, those two. If they shifted into anything, it might be a couple of old cats, purring on a sunny windowsill.

Tina, though, she could picture turning into a sleek fox with a beautiful ebony sheen. Make that a crafty fox. Because for all that Tina sat quietly, Stef suspected something was up. Not that she didn't trust Tina—the woman seemed genuine enough, just as everyone on the ranch seemed to be. But in the meetings yesterday, Tina seemed every bit a part of the leadership team as her brothers. So what was she doing, touring a stranger around the ranch and lingering over lunch?

When Tina glanced at her watch and suddenly declared it time to get going, Stef was sure she'd been stalling all along. The question was, stalling for what?

She had her answer shortly after they thanked the older women and turned a corner to the central square of the ranch. A group of men was just filing out of the council house. Meeting adjourned?

Stef pulled up short as a wave of anger stiffened her spine. "So, they've finished deliberating my case?"

Tina turned, a shadow of guilt veiling her eyes. "It's not like that."

"Then what is it like? Tell me."

The others were coming up now: Cody, with a sunny expression that didn't quite reach his eyes, along with a tight-lipped Ty and two others she didn't recognize. Behind them, Kyle emerged from the council house looking like a man blindsided by a surprise verdict. Her heart sang on seeing him but clenched on reading that look.

"It's complicated," Tina started.

Stefanie all but bared her teeth as the men came up to face her. "Try me."

Tina exchanged looks with Ty and Cody, and Stef could sense words flying though no one spoke. More secrets?

"Tell me!"

It was Cody who finally met her eyes and spoke. "Look, we want to help you, we really do."

Not a promising prelude. A twitch started in her left eye.

"This is the thing," Cody continued as Kyle came up and locked his eyes on hers.

His face wore an expression she knew all too well from the old days: the same bitter look that followed one of his stepfather's rampages. The look that said he had to accept his fate, much as he despised it.

Cody was going on, explaining that they couldn't shelter her on the ranch for fear of trouble on a larger scale. Something about shifter laws that forbade one pack from harboring a fugitive from another. "And technically," Cody added, "you're a fugitive."

She threw up her hands. "Technically?" She hammered the man with a glare that held all her pent-up frustration. "Technically?" Then she stomped off, leaving Cody protesting behind her.

"We have a solution, though," he called. "There's another pack, a hundred miles west—"

"So glad you've figured everything out for me," she shot over her shoulder and hurried away. They'd been stringing her along, all this time. They were shipping her out to her fate.

She clenched her hands into fists, but then jerked them apart at a jab of pain. It felt like her fingernails were being pulled out by the roots.

She paled. Were those claws in there, ready to break free? The rage she felt was far, far more intense than anything she'd ever felt before.

At the sound of footsteps, she spun, not sure whether she could keep the wolf locked away. Not even sure if she cared.

It was Kyle, though, not Cody or Tina, and the rage receded just as quickly as it had come. He looked worn and weary, a decade older than the day before. "Hey."

"Hey," she whispered, cocking her head at him. "You okay?"

Kyle shoved his lower jaw sideways on its hinge and grunted a reply. "Yeah. Good."

The man looked like he'd been pushing boulders up a mountain all night, only to have them roll straight down again. The blue of his eyes was a little pale, his look equal parts exhaustion and determination. The familiar look of a kid fighting impossible odds and refusing to give up. Before she could process her own thoughts, she had her arms around him, squeezing tight. It was a desperate, crazy gesture, but his arms went around her too, and she breathed him in, pulling great, long gasps of his scent into her lungs. He seemed to be doing the same, pulling her ever closer, refusing to let them be torn apart in the hurricane that was about to strike.

She melted into him, and he tilted his head into hers, murmuring something undecipherable in low, scratchy tones. Then he shuddered, perhaps recalling some awful truth, and pulled away. He gazed at her quietly before smoothing a lock of hair behind her ear.

"So now what do I do?" she whispered.

His hands ran along her arms as he took a deep breath. "Do you trust me?"

Did he have to ask?

He took her hand and led her back to the others. There was a short standoff in which Stefanie feared Cody would start up again with that hypnotizing tenor of his. But Kyle squeezed her hand and started first.

"She comes with me." It was a statement, not a suggestion.

Ty immediately started to bristle, but Cody protested first. "If she stays on the ranch, we're in violation of pack law—"

"If she stays with me," Kyle broke in, "she's not on the ranch. Technically."

Stef watched the three siblings exchange glances. Tina was the first to tilt her head sideways. "True, the old blacksmith's place is on a separate parcel..."

"I don't like it," Ty barked.

"Could work, though, as a temporary solution," Cody conceded.

Stef's heart jerked at the word *temporary*, but she kept her mouth shut.

Tina went on, nodding to herself. "It's far enough not to flaunt pack laws, but close enough in case..."

Everyone went silent, and Stefanie wasn't sure she wanted to fill in the blanks. Ty gave a slow nod, and she could read the message in his eyes. The one aimed at Kyle.

Do not fuck this up.

She looked from face to face, wanting to plead her case, but the distant sound of a child's laughter pulled everyone's attention away. She turned, letting her eyes drift over the ranch as the laugh rang out again, followed by the eager woof of a dog, both somewhere out of sight.

And just like that, she understood.

There was peace and continuity here on the ranch. Life. Love. Prosperity. She glanced at the ranch leaders, seeing them in a new light. Human or not, they were good at heart, and they had a lot to lose by getting embroiled in a battle that wasn't theirs.

And yet they were offering to help. Even if it was temporary, she'd take it.

She felt herself swaying again, losing resolve. Because really, what else could she do but heed their word? She'd never felt so powerless in her life.

Until Kyle nudged her and caught hold of her with those deep blue eyes. There was her answer. He'd been powerless, too, once upon a time, and yet he'd moved on. Kyle was living proof that there were ways to overcome.

Though Ty was scrubbing his jaw, clearly unhappy with the solution, he did manage to give her a bolstering nod. Cody was smiling—a real smile this time. Tina was swinging her eyes back and forth between Stef and Kyle, analyzing them closely.

Stef shivered, wondering what Tina saw in her. A raving lunatic? A rabid animal? A lost soul?

"Come on," Kyle said, tugging her hand.

She took a deep breath. It was time to take action for herself, even if it was only the first crawling inch toward an uncertain destination. One shaky step toward Kyle's truck at a time. Her legs grew bolder when he swung in step beside her, and then she was climbing into the high cab and leaning over to open his door before buckling herself in. And there it was again, his scent, filling her with hope. The engine roared to life, and they were off, rolling under the ranch gateway and out into the desert.

Just the two of them. Alone.

Chapter Twelve

Stefanie tried to process her dark new reality of packs, mates, and unwritten laws during the drive home.

Home. She snorted. Her home was a sparsely furnished rental apartment in Colorado, but she couldn't go there. She doubted the neighbors even noticed her absence. And anyway, the North Ridge wolves would find her there.

Wolves don't give up on mates, Tina had said.

She watched the prickly pear and cactus blur past for a few minutes, wondering whether the North Ridge wolves could find her here. The open desert wasn't like the woods when it came to places to hide.

What had Ty and Cody promised?

We'll help to whatever degree we can.

She had to wonder what degree that might be.

Kyle might have been thinking the same thing, the way he was flexing and re-flexing his fingers around the steering wheel. If push did come to shove, where would he stand? More importantly, could she even ask him—or any of them—to take a stand? After all, the mess she was in was all her fault.

She tilted her head back against the headrest and closed her eyes, listening to the steady roll of the tires, searching for some source of comfort. Kyle's hug had been more than just a hug of reassurance, and the scent slowly tickling her nose now was about more than a place to crash for a couple of nights. That much was clear, even to her untrained sense of smell. She drifted off, wondering why she welcomed the possibilities so keenly.

Then there was a lurch, and she snapped her chin up, suddenly awake. Her lips parted in an instinctive smile at the sight

67

of his house, the shed out back, the creaky old windmill up on a rise. Somehow, it felt more right than anything on the ranch. More like home.

But when her eyes found Kyle's, expecting to find a similar kind of relief, there was only the cold touch of steel.

"I have to go," he grunted.

Go? Where? She blinked as his gaze slid to the car door, hinting that she should get out. He'd left the engine running, too.

A sticky lump formed in her throat. Her friend was gone, replaced by a stranger with cool, military eyes. Eyes that reminded her of her father's or brother's when they were getting ready to ship out.

"Where are you going?" she squeaked.

"Work."

The man whose eyes had promised her the world suddenly couldn't do better than four letters, one curt syllable, and a kick out the door. What happened? Had she done something wrong?

She found the door handle more by touch than sight, her vision blurred by tears she fought to hold back. She slid out of the truck, swayed a little when she touched down, then pushed the truck door closed.

Before she even made it to the porch, Kyle drove off, leaving a plume of dust and a rutted wake of gravel. She sank down on the top step and watched him go. The hard-to-read kid had become a walking hieroglyph. Earlier in the day, he'd been her shining knight, her savior. Now, he couldn't seem to get away from her fast enough.

She sat there a long time, clasping and unclasping her hands until something niggled at her senses. She stood and walked to a corner of the porch. A nearly full moon was rapidly clawing its way from behind the hills, swinging on a seesaw with the sun. The minute the sun set, the moon would take over and fill the sky with its pale light.

The hair on the back of her neck shivered, and Stef hugged herself tightly.

Chapter Thirteen

Kyle had to admit that work was a lame excuse. But a minute longer in Stef's company and he might have done something he'd regret, like following that enticing scent straight to her neck. The way she'd tipped her head back in the truck had pulled every trigger in his body. She was so innocent. So trusting.

So sweet.

Yeah, that was the wolf again, and the beast was getting harder and harder to control.

He'd been tracing her slight curves with this eyes, studying the athletic figure. The tomboy had filled out in all the right places without overflowing awkwardly into a body that didn't match her soul. He wanted to reach out and feel her heat—a heat that pulsed and flared whenever they got close.

Mine! Mate! His wolf leaped straight up, practically salivating.

He could feel the beast trying to break free even after he put some miles between them. Goddamn wolf was already planning the bite, calculating just where to place each fang and how must pressure it would take to puncture her skin— gently, ever so gently. His fangs would bore deep, and then close tight, sealing a clean mating bite that would secure her forever. As his.

We take her! Now!

Even his human side was half in agreement. *One bite turns, the second bite mates.* He knew it as well as any other shifter. A mating bite from him would cancel out Ron's initial claim. Stefanie would be his, and his alone.

Greed burned in his throat, and it was all he could do to wrestle it back down.

Claiming her now would make us as low as Ron, he told the wolf. *She has to want it too.*

She wants it! Her wolf wants it!

He shook his head. She had to understand the implications. That it meant forever. With him. With his wolf.

And Christ, why would she ever say yes to that?

She'd always seen him as a lost puppy who needed rescuing, nothing more.

That's not the vibe I got from her today, man.

He had to wonder what she was rescuing him from now. He'd pushed away the past, made a decent life for himself. Had a good job and a pack that accepted him. He didn't need any rescuing now.

Except maybe from yourself, the wolf sniffed.

His soul was a candle burning at both ends, and he knew it. The human side fizzled at one end, lost and lonely as he'd ever been, and his wolf blazed at the other, desperate for acceptance.

She can fix that candle. Make it burn bright.

Kyle slammed a door on his wolf and drove on. But even when he merged on to the highway twenty minutes later, the wolf was still whimpering for her. Images of Stef chased him all the way to headquarters and up the stairs, straight past the dispatcher who looked up in surprise.

"Kyle! What are you doing in today?"

He grunted something neutral and climbed the stairs in jerky, robotic steps then sat at his desk to shuffle a few reports. Stefanie's scent clung to his clothes like a burr, and he almost wished for the radio to crackle with a crisis of some kind. Gang activity to crack down on, maybe, or a drug bust. Anything to distract him. But the citizens of central Arizona were behaving themselves and things were quiet. It always was this time of year.

"Officer Williams." A familiar voice broke into the room, followed by the clink of keys tossed on the neighboring desk.

He looked up to see two of his colleagues coming in, ready to wrap up their shift.

"Don't you have something better to do on your day off?" Lee chided.

"Days off," the other, Chavez, said. "The man has a week off. Me, I'd be out of here."

Kyle responded with his usual line of defense: silence.

"You're the only person I know who has to be ordered to take his vacation days." Chavez shook his head. "Do you even know what a vacation is? Va-ca-tion?"

Kyle straightened his back but said nothing. He didn't need a vacation. He'd wandered enough in his life.

"Aw, come on, leave the guy in peace." That was Andie—Andrea—another colleague, just coming in the door. Kyle threw her an appreciative nod. She was one of the best officers on the force and one of the few people who left him in peace.

"What he needs," Chavez said with a waggle of his bushy eyebrows, "is a woman." The other two grunted their disapproval, but Chavez went on, waving his hands. "All the man has to do is spend three minutes in a bar and they're on him like flies on a carcass. Me, I'd be taking them home."

Kyle pressed his lips into a tight line. He did have a woman at home. One he didn't know what to make of.

I know what to make her, his wolf hummed smugly. *Mine. Mate.*

If he could have physically cuffed the beast, he would have. He didn't need a mate. Didn't need anyone. There was no such thing as destiny—not for humans, nor for wolves. And definitely not for him.

Lee tried a new tack. "You need to get away from work for a while."

Kyle shook his head. Work was as good a place as any. It filled the holes in his life. Some of them, anyway.

"Guys, give it up." Andie sighed from behind the stack of files on her desk.

"Or you could fix something at home," Lee went on. "You know, put up a shed or something. That's what you need, a home improvement project."

Kyle held back a snort. Home. Where was that?

The pack is our home, his wolf snipped.

Kyle gave a mental shake of the head. The pack was only half a home. He had a little too much human in him to fit in at the ranch and a little too much wolf for a life outside it. But he'd found his niche, and things were fine the way they were.

At least they had been until Stefanie came along, stirring up all kinds of crazy thoughts. Like the urge to possess, to protect. To hunt the bastard who'd attacked her and rip him into tiny little bits. He knew the others had glossed over the details, keeping the worst of it from her. Sooner or later, the North Ridge wolves would come to claim her. Much as his packmates sympathized with Stefanie, they wouldn't defy pack law for her. That bastard Ron had turned her. He'd have first rights to claim her, too.

His inner wolf snarled. *Let him try.*

He tried not to picture it, but the ugly images were impossible to lock out. Stefanie being dragged off against her will. She'd learned to fight somewhere along the line, but her lean, five-foot-eight frame was no match for a hungry male. He pictured a he-wolf pinning her down and twisting her head sideways to expose her throat. Forcing the mating bite then forcing the rest of his body on her, into her. Even a woman as tough as Stef couldn't resist the power of a mating bond. She'd be a prisoner, a slave, a shadow of herself. She'd be Ron's. Forever.

"Earth to Williams. Hello."

Something snapped, and Kyle looked down to find a crushed pencil in his hand. He dropped the pieces in disgust. Why couldn't he turn on the same cool reasoning he did with any other criminal case?

"Man, you really do need a vacation."

And once again, the memories flooded in. Pleasant ones he didn't know he had. A thousand images of Stefanie in motion. The girl was always loping off to some sports practice or another. Soccer, he remembered, and basketball and track. She'd thrown herself at sports like she might find a second family out on a field or in a gym. With an ailing mother, an ambitious brother, and a father who rotated in and out of active deployments, Stef must have had her own closet of fears. Fears that had come true, because she wouldn't have come running into the desert if she'd had family to turn to.

She'd like belonging to a pack, his wolf decided. *An honest pack like Twin Moon.*

"Someday..." He remembered her whispering to him after one of his stepfather's rampages. Like there really was a someday out there and it would be better.

Then one day, the tomboy next door was gone, off to her father's new posting, and someday got buried under an avalanche of ugly memories.

Someday. Kyle had given up hope for anything like that. And now, Stefanie brought it all back.

But hope was a dangerous thing, especially for a hopeless case like him.

Chapter Fourteen

Stef wandered around the house then shut herself in the spare bedroom she'd changed in before—the pink one on the east side, a throw-back to the 70s that she imagined belonged to the daughter of the previous owners. The window opened on a view of the old windmill, standing as silent and gaping as a skeleton. The moon had just cleared the hills, fat and greedy and ready to take over the night.

Her skin itched just looking at it. It itched from the inside. *The need will start to pull you in.*

She pulled the blinds and fretted before flopping on the bed with a magazine she'd pulled from the heap in the living room. A minute later, she was up again, pacing her cage. The room was cramped, the air stale. The window beckoned, but she resisted the urge to throw it open and lean out. Who knew what the desert air might bring to her tonight: nightmares or fantasies?

She tried to force her eyes back to Kyle's magazine—*Law Enforcement Today*—but it was no good. Slowly, inexorably, the moon song found her until the urge to respond became a command. The pale light seemed to pulse right into the room, right in time with the throbbing of the wound on her neck.

Skinwalker. The terrified eyes of the Navajo woman shone in her memory.

She jumped up and bolted the door, more to keep herself in than to keep something out.

Hot and stuffy became a sauna, a coffin. She pulled off layer after layer until all she wore were her panties and bra. Maybe the choking feeling would pass, just as it had on the previous nights when the same symptoms appeared: the sweaty face, the prickly skin, the cramped muscles. Each time, the feeling had gradually ceased.

Or had it? That was the blurry part of her memory. A few nights ago, she'd dreamed she was dying, the pain in her joints was so intense. She'd lain crying and panting on the bed of a cheap motel, thinking that was it. One minute, the clock was showing midnight and she was in agony; the next, the birds were singing in the dawn. Everything in between was a blur of sound, scents, and sensations that might not even have been her own. Panting breaths. A lolling tongue. The beat of a four-footed run. The call of the wild in her bones.

Let me out.

It was a whisper, and it came from inside.

"No way." She curled into a tighter ball and started rocking herself. Was she going crazy?

Not crazy, said a contralto voice that was both foreign and familiar.

"Kyle." She whimpered his name, and a series of memories flashed through her mind. Him as a kid, him as an adult. Steady. Solid. Secure.

Except Kyle wasn't here now, and suddenly, she couldn't take it any more.

In a heated rush, she dashed for the door, fumbled it open, and plunged into the dark pool of night. The world was spinning and she stood at the center, watching the universe go round and round while her lungs heaved desperately for a breath of air. A thousand stars swirled, and she almost laughed at the vision from Van Gogh.

There was a dizzying thrill to it at first, but then the pain took over. The change.

It began with a massive yawn that ripped through her face, unhinging her jaw. Her body contorted, stretching wildly until she collapsed to her hands and knees, moaning at the tearing sensation inside. Her stomach was being pulled down, her lungs up. Her knees were popping, her skin burning.

Let me out.

She wanted to dig in her heels and push back, as if she were battling an overstuffed closet about to burst open and release a deluge. A monster.

I am not a monster. I am you.

Her eyes flashed and color leached out of her vision until all she could see between frantic blinks was a world of black, white, and a million grays. Sound and smell rushed in and intensified, filling her nose with a thousand overpowering scents and her ears with tones much higher or lower than she should have been able to register. The quiet desert had become rush hour in the city: the faintest rustle of bushes became a din, the chirp of insects a riot. And under it all, like the deepest bass drum, was that irresistible moon song.

Let me out. You'll see.

She squeezed her eyes tighter, shuddering. She didn't want to see anything.

The wracking stretch of her body went impossibly far and her joints strained, slipping out of whack. Her jaw hung open in a silent scream as her shoulder blades pulled back much, much farther than they ought to be able to go. Her heart beat wildly. Any minute, it would burst and the world would go black.

Except it didn't. The pain went on and on, and she dragged herself along the ground. An oversized coat had been thrown over her body; it clung tight in her armpits but shifted loosely along her back. A twig broke somewhere on her right, and that sent her skittering away. But her feet kept tangling with her arms, and she fell. It was only when she realized she was on all fours that she managed to coordinate her limbs. She ran on four clumsy feet, trying to escape the truth.

Skinwalker.

Shifter.

Wolf.

The beast that had stolen her body gobbled up its newfound freedom, relishing its power and speed. Her human mind became a distant observer, watching in terrified fascination. She was a wolf. A wild beast. Would she go on a bloody rampage, tearing livestock limb from limb? Haunt the hills with a mournful howl then slink into a den?

The wolf gave a violent shake that started at the nose and ended at the tail.

Tail?

The beast did it a second time, just for the satisfaction of having won control. Then it set off in a crazy dance, reveling in its body and the light of the moon. It set off a hum inside that even her human side wanted to sing right back to.

Awaroooo...

The wolf lifted its muzzle and began to sing, adding its voice to the choir of the night.

Aaaaarrrrroooo....

The sound resonated in her chest and echoed through the night.

Images came with the sound. Images of a dozen canine feet pounding the ground, then huddling on a hilltop and singing this song. She'd lean against one—and not just any one, but the brown wolf with spiky hair and sharp blue eyes—and howl her soul out into the night. Sing until all the doubt was gone and hope had filled back in.

Unlike the blur of the previous nights, this night was cool, sharp, and clear. Every breath, every step a thrill. Her wolf was high, giggling, gloriously one with the night. A wisp of human awareness fought it all, but the wolf beat it back.

We're one, silly. Stop fighting me.

Stef wanted to shake her head, but part of her was already giving in.

Watch. Learn. Listen.

If she still had hands, she'd have held them over her ears.

Listen, the wolf insisted, and its voice grew more urgent. *Listen to the night. The warning.*

The beast cocked its head, lifted its ears, and Stef had no choice but to tune in.

The beating bass drum of the moon formed the underlying pulse of the night. But under it—no, behind it, beyond the horizon—came a faint metallic tap along with a tobacco-laced scent.

Her wolf froze when she recognized it. Ron. Honing in on her.

Ron. Coming to claim.

She could have screamed until she was hoarse, but the only sound that emerged was a canine snarl.

Watch. Listen. Be warned.

Chapter Fifteen

Lee and Chavez were still droning on as Kyle worked his jaw back and forth, fighting memories away.

And not just memories. He was getting totally inappropriate fantasies, too. Like holding Stefanie closer than close. Peeling off layers of denim and cotton to touch her, taste her, bury himself in her. To let instinct take over and make them both howl in sweaty pleasure. But Jesus, it wasn't right to think thoughts like those, not about the girl next door.

Except that the wolf liked those thoughts. He liked them very much.

The first weeks as a Changeling—for those who survived, anyway—could wreak havoc on the body. That was probably what his wolf was responding to. Right?

His wolf grunted and flopped to the floor in his mental doghouse. *When are you going to get it, man?*

There was nothing to get. Emotion couldn't have anything to do with it. He wouldn't let it, damn it! Because he didn't want or need anyone. And neither did Stefanie. All she needed was to get out of this mess.

So he'd help her, damn it. He'd see her through this, and then send her off to make a new life for herself. One he wouldn't have a part in, because why would she want him?

"Get out of this office before the chief sees you, man," Lee persisted.

Kyle gave him the evil eye, wishing they'd stop harping on him. Work was all he had. All he wanted.

"Hey, Kyle." That was Andie, and her voice was soft. "You really ought to take a break."

He'd give himself a break when Stef was safe, and not a minute sooner.

"Sure," he mumbled, making for the door.

Lee was right. The office wasn't what he needed, so he left, briefly considering Chavez's advice to head to a bar and let a woman take him to bed. That would work off some of the wolf's misplaced energy. It had been a while since he'd cruised the bars—since his drinking buddy, Cody, had given up the playboy act for a mate and the role he was born to: second-in-command of Twin Moon pack. But Kyle had no such responsibilities. Why not make up for lost time?

The answer came right on the heels of the question. It wasn't *why not* but *why*? He didn't want just any woman. Didn't want a superficial thrill.

He blinked at the roads and found himself heading home. To her.

To her, his wolf agreed.

When he pulled up at his house twenty minutes later, the beast was practically wagging his tail. But the minute he got one foot out the car door, he froze. The scent of wolf was everywhere. The scent of danger.

His wolf almost tore out of his skin then and there, though he forced a slow 360-degree turn first, sniffing the air. A moment later, he did the same in wolf form, drawing in the scent, ready to hunt the intruder and make him pay. The saliva was already building behind his growl and his hair was standing on end.

As his nose dissected the scent, though, he found it familiar.

Pleasing. Feminine.

His curse came out as a low bark. That wolf was Stefanie, and she was gone.

In a flash, the anger coursing through him flipped right over to fear. Where was she? Was she all right? Not every human could survive the first shift and become a full were. All along he'd been putting the thought off, counting on Stef to be strong enough to be the exception. But now that it had happened, he was seized with doubt. Jesus, what if she didn't make it?

He sprinted off, tracking the fresh trail, crazy with fear. He remembered the shock of his first transformation, the tearing physical pain. He'd been by turns suicidal and homicidal his first few times, consumed by the uncontrollable urges splitting his mind. Would Stefanie be the same? Maybe it would be even worse for her. Maybe she'd fold under the pressure...

He remembered the voices that had whispered over his prone form when he'd first come to the ranch, an utter wreck.

A Changeling.

Christ, what a mess.

Will he make it?

Unlikely. They hardly ever do.

Someone had kicked the dirt and sighed.

They hardly ever do.

He thundered past a briar patch, ignoring the thorns ripping at his fur. What the hell had he been thinking, leaving Stef alone on a full moon? He should have stayed and helped her through the night. He couldn't count the times she'd hunkered down with him as a kid, the number of secrets she'd kept for him. There'd been at least one for every bruise his stepfather put on his body.

And yet when she needed him most, he'd run away.

He charged through the night, chasing unbearable images. Like Stefanie, unable to handle the shift and going feral, a mad wolf that would have to be hunted and killed. Or Stef, lying dead because her body fought the transition too hard.

He came to a skidding halt on the next rise, spotting a soft shape curled by a boulder halfway down the slope. He shuffled forward toward the brown-beige wolf and sniffed anxiously. It was her, his brown-eyed girl. Except those eyes were closed, the breathing shallow. Her heartbeat was a faint tap in the night. He licked her muzzle then curled his body around hers, desperate for some sign that she was all right. But there was no sign, only that faint, distant beat. All he could do was keep her close. He puffed out his fur, trapping warm air and doing his best to block out the moonlight along with dark thoughts.

What if she died? What if she failed to recover? What if?

Chapter Sixteen

Stefanie found herself floating unsteadily over the desert land-scape, knowing it was a dream. Something tickled her nostrils, though, and that part felt real. She wrinkled her nose, wishing reality away. Drifting in a void was preferable to facing the harsh truth.

Like wolf. Werewolf.

With a snort and a sneeze, she tried to settle back into nothingness, but something pulled her back. Even through the haze that clogged her mind, she knew something was different. The desert had gone silent again. The moon had rolled to the other side of the sky, pulling the constellations with it. Color filled in her vision again while her other senses had gone dull. Her fingertips were cold, trembling.

Fingers. Hands. She blinked, holding them up.

Human.

She was herself again, curled in a ball. Shivering. The wolf that had taken over was gone. She didn't know whether she should cry with relief or scream her sorrow into the night. All that came were tears that welled up from a deep, dark place of doubt. They spilled down her cheeks as her breath came out in great, choking sobs that protested what had been forced upon her. She wasn't herself any more. The crushing emptiness of night weighed down on her as she lay lost and alone.

Except she wasn't alone. A strong, safe something cov-ered her back, and she knew without looking that it was Kyle, wrapped around her like a winter coat.

"Hey," he whispered, again and again. "You're okay."

He must have been there a while because that hug was warmer than five or ten minutes old. How long didn't matter and neither did how. Only that she wasn't alone.

"It's okay."

She cried in sorrow and relief until the wracking sobs wore themselves out and she could match her breathing to the rise and fall of his chest. He was warm and hard but soft, too, that outer layer of pliant skin backed by a foundation of steely muscle, all of it molded carefully to her lines. For a short time at least, she could pretend something about this was normal. Never mind that she was up a mountainside in the dark. Never mind that she was wrapped in a stranger's arms.

No, not a stranger. A friend. An old friend. She was herself again, and everything was all right. The stars shining brightly overhead told her so. They had that look again, like she'd hit the angle on them just right.

So right, in fact, that when the gradual awareness that she was naked, and Kyle was too, set in, it soothed instead of frightened and set off a low thrum in her core. She turned and slid along his body until her face was hidden in his neck. The jagged line of his scars pressed into her bare skin, but even that felt good. Fresh and homey, he smelled like sage and sunflower intertwined.

Her fingers stroked his chest, her chin tilted up, and it was the most natural thing in the world to lift and kiss.

His lips were as soft as his body was hard, and it was just like her dream in the guesthouse: that feeling of sliding into a deep, warm bath. Nudging closer, she followed the blind, building need. Her tongue traced the line of his teeth, and yes, they were as perfectly straight as they looked. She lifted her eyes and found Kyle's eyes alive with flashes of gold.

Friend, she thought. *So good to have a friend.*

Mate, said a whisper, a voice in the night.

Claim! added a husky contralto she suspected might be the wolf.

"Kyle," she whispered, and even his name felt perfect on her lips.

The gold hadn't been in his eyes when she'd known him before. Whatever it was, it came out with extremes. When he was angry, frustrated, thrilled. Or like now: aroused. She could smell it, see it, taste it on his lips, even though she sensed him trying to beat it back. Because he was a friend; because of that beautifully outdated honor code of his.

"Kyle." She pushed closer, suddenly giving in to a rush of frustration. For the past week, her life had been wildly out of control. Now, everything became the here, the now, the him.

His lips were moving but failing to form words, his body radiating heat. She couldn't stop herself from straddling his hips. Her mouth closed over his, desperately seeking with her tongue. Seeking and finding some tiny grain of truth—that they belonged together. That this heat building between them was a sign that everything would be all right.

She rocked over him. Full and thick, his cock pulsed against her sex and an overwhelming craving for more consumed her. Kyle groaned beneath her—a low, straining sound that said he wanted this as much as she did. She pushed her breasts into his chest, settled deeper into his lap, and stroked her tongue over his lips. What would it take to unravel this man?

"Kyle, please," she begged, and didn't even berate herself for her weakness. Weakness was crying; strength was the ability to ask for what she needed.

Him.

She turned her lips on his ear, and a shudder went through him. Kyle pulled back just long enough to give her one smoldering look then smothered her lips with his, ravaging her mouth with an intensity that rivaled hers. When his hand swept up her body and cupped a breast, she trembled. Willing him to take the next step, she rocked her hips over his, trying to latch on to him. Letting body language do the begging.

Please. Now. Take me. Because not having him now would shatter her. She'd suffered through a crazy week alone, and now all she wanted was him.

Mate. Claim!

He dipped his head to her breast and the moist contact was like a kiss to the soul. The rub of his thumb dialed up her desire, and she swore her nipples would jump right off her body. He could swallow them whole, nibble them up, and she still wouldn't get enough.

Oh God, she was wet. Wet and aching for that moment when two became one.

"Stef," Kyle whispered. His lips tickled her ear. "Be sure."

"I'm sure. Believe me, I'm sure."

She nibbled on his jaw, his ear, his lower lip. In a week of being sure of nothing, he was her shining light.

He pulled back and looked into her eyes so long, she swore she might find her climax in the golden-edged blue. Even more so when he inched his hand between them and cupped her mound.

She couldn't help it; she had to cry his name. Had to tell him how good it felt to have him this close. How desperate she was to find more than a friend on this lonely desert night. She would have begged if he hadn't slipped a finger between her folds then dragged it forward to find her clit. The man was driving her right up a spiral staircase to the top floor.

"You like that." A statement, not a question.

She couldn't respond, except in short syllables in her mind. *More. Need. Inside.*

He pushed a finger inside her and immediately added a second. She was that wide, that ready. Her back was arched so far back, her fingers barely touched his shoulders. His left hand held her tightly while his right worked its magic. She peeked and found his face intent, like he was taking a test instead of getting her off. Like he wanted to get it exactly right.

"You like this?" he whispered.

"God, I love that."

Didn't he know he couldn't fail? Not with her. Never. He'd always been like that, though. Supremely confident in some things, ridiculously anxious about a handful of secret weaknesses.

She thought the rumble she heard was him, but the quiet space between two breaths said it was her—or the wolf in her. She shivered, half thrilled, half afraid.

"Kyle. I need you."

His lips went tight, but his eyes said, *I need you. I want you.*

She rode his hand until her insides were twisted so tight, she couldn't take it any more. With an insistent nudge of the hips, she pushed straight past his hand and toward his cock, grinding onto him.

She cried out as his thick cock slid inside and barely registered his husky *Yes*. Every muscle in her body went limp except those sheathing him now, because that was all that mattered.

Kyle pushed up into her, and it was like he'd take her to the stars. Once, twice, lifting her gently, then urging her back down in ever harder jerks.

"Stef..." He broke off whatever he was going to say and clamped his hands over her hips. The world tilted as he lifted and turned them both, putting her back on the ground. When they bottomed out, he pushed so deep, she cried out at the searing pleasure-pain.

Kyle threw his head back and savored whatever it was she managed to make him feel. Needed? Wanted? Or maybe just on fire?

"You like that." It was her turn to steal that line.

The golden sparks rocketing in his eyes said, *Fuck yes, I do*.

Then he fell into a rhythm he might have kept up forever. The couple of other men she'd slept with would have been long spent by now, snoring or lumbering off to the bathroom, but he was only now building to a climax.

The ground beneath her was cool; everything above was a pure, raging heat, and she arched into it. His eyes glowed as he pushed again and again. Stef wanted to stretch this exquisite high out forever, but the beast within was clawing, begging for more.

Yes, yes, yes!

She couldn't have him fast enough, hard enough, deep enough, and she cried for more until he was hammering hard. A wave built inside, one she was desperate to hold back yet eager to release. Then she was rocking wildly, crying out when the crest broke inside. A second later, Kyle grunted and a slick inner heat engulfed her. For a moment, they paused, eyes locked; then she closed her eyes on an aftershock and clamped over him one last time. Kyle gave a choking groan and pushed back, lifting her into one final, roaring high. Then they were both limp and panting, their bodies one in the night.

"Jesus, Stef..."

Yeah, he liked it all right, her inner voice said with a grin.

She closed her eyes to the surrounding scrub, the vastness of the desert, the glorious night sky. To everything but the feeling of belonging. Here. Now. With him.

Chapter Seventeen

Mate. My mate.

Kyle heard the words ring in his mind. They took on shape and weight, growing to an insistent chorus of voices that rose as one from the land.

He swore he could feel her heart beat in exact time with his.

Mate, sang the alto of the stars. *Mate,* boomed the low bass of the hills. He imagined a wolf spirit emerging from a hollow and urging him to mark her, promising if he would, everything would be all right. Everything would fit, these scattered jigsaw pieces of his life.

He pushed back her hair, stroking her neck, and Jesus, she purred. That was him, doing that to her. That was a thrill completely unlike the hangover feeling of being with a woman who didn't see who he really was. This was Stef, and her eyes promised him that the useless punching bag of a kid was different. Special.

Maybe even worthy.

Mate! His wolf honed in on the exact spot on her neck.

Right there, instinct said, *just beside the pulse in the hollow under her chin.*

Right there was his ticket to escape. Hers, too, because his bite would bond them forever and sever Ron's tenuous hold.

He had heard about mating bites for as long as he'd been in the pack, and it always sounded so risky, so gory. Now, it seemed easy. One jaw there, the other there, and a gentle push. A squeeze to maintain the seal on her artery and keep her safe while his system imprinted the essence of her. Then

91

he'd withdraw so slowly that the wound would heal on the spot.

It didn't seem scary. It seemed just right.

He leaned in, sniffing the spot, then warmed it with his tongue as his canines started to extend. Stef's inner wolf gave a barely audible moan.

Take me. Have me, my mate.

He was just readying for the bite when an owl hooted, and the sound stopped him cold.

Why the hell are you stopping? his wolf shouted in his mind.

Her wolf might want the bite, but her human side wasn't ready.

She's ready, man! his wolf insisted.

Only her body.

That's enough.

He shook his head at the beast. No, it wasn't. Not yet. She needed to be ready with all her soul. She'd already been savaged by a stranger, and this moment was too delicate to mar with a bite. He swallowed hard, coaxing his canines back into his gums, then snuggled Stef closer. It wasn't a night for claiming. It was a night to hold, to kiss, to comfort.

His wolf snorted. *You mean her doing that to you, or you doing that to her?*

A warm, pleasant haze fell over him. Fate skipped past on a tumbleweed, unthreatening, unconcerned. He could stay wrapped in this woman's body forever. Because Stef didn't judge, didn't push, didn't demand. She was just there for him, as she always had been. And if words like love, fate, and destiny usually had him smirking—*yeah, right*—tonight he let them soak into him like a balm.

But night and bare human skin didn't mix—not for long, anyway. When Stef shivered, he stood and offered her a hand up, quietly admiring the smooth lines of her body. It was just like seeing her come out of the house earlier that day, freshly showered. She had an air about her, a glow, like she'd shed a layer of emotional grime and brought her inner beauty closer to the surface.

Naked, side by side with her, winding home, he should have felt awkward, but it felt so right. The way was long and slow in bare human feet, but she walked silently, warm hand clasped in his. That was new. Not just walking hand in hand with a woman—because what kind of pansy-ass romantic did that?—but walking hand in hand with Stef.

His wolf seconded the sentiment with a possessive growl he couldn't quite hold back.

She turned, eyes swirling with color. "Hmmm?"

"Nothing," he mumbled, gripping her hand tighter and wondering why it didn't feel weird. Shouldn't they be kicking a ball to each other, chewing gum, comparing bubbles? He studied her profile, bathed in moonlight. No, he decided. The kids were in the past. This new and very grown-up thing was his present. Hell, maybe even his future.

Kyle sucked his lower lip, thinking that one over as he walked. There were a million complications to that scenario—starting with a shit of a wolf named Ron and his badass alpha, Greer. Too many variables he couldn't control. Working criminal cases for the state was much easier than this. He could stay detached, cool, professional. With Stef, though... Well, the night was proof he hadn't been anything close to detached or cool or professional.

Not detached. Attached. His wolf grinned. *Tell me you didn't like that?*

They were a mess of sweat, burrs, and dust by the time they reached the bottom stair of his porch. They'd been ambling along like the outside world didn't exist, but shit, there was his truck and his house, telling them it did. His chest tightened, knowing that any moment, she might pull away and end this magical night.

"Kyle," she started.

Not a protest. A plea.

Her hand was stroking his back, and before either of them moved one inch closer to rational thought, he pulled her against his chest and claimed her mouth in a hurricane of a kiss. A triumphant flash hammered his body when her tongue reached back for his, hungering for more.

He got lost in her so quickly, so hopelessly, that when the porch step creaked under them, he wondered if it was a warning. Was he letting himself feel too much, too fast? But there was no fighting this insatiable thirst, and all he could do was quench it—or at least try. Stef tasted of everything good: like warm milk, an innocent pleasure from a long time ago, back to comfort him with its familiar flavor one more time.

They got as far as the top step before folding into each other again, letting quiet coos and gentle touches escalate into a breathless blur. For a while, she took the length of him in her hand and stroked with a rhythm no woman had ever gifted him with before. It was all he could do to hold back a tremble and eventually pull away. This night was about her, not him. He kissed her deep and long then eased her back. His heart was racing at the sight of her, laid out before him like a feast.

His wolf licked his lips.

Her, not you, he told the beast.

Sure, man. Anything you say.

He kneeled before her and fluttered kisses down her body, all the way down to her mound. She was holding her breath, and hell, he was too, at the threshold to her private world. He spread her wide, and what was intended as a gentle kiss turned into a greedy lick when the flavor of her rocketed through his nerves. He circled the nub of her clit then sucked. Hard.

A spasm went through her, and though her eyes were shining with surprise when he glanced up, she spread her legs wider, begging for more. He wanted to freeze the moment in a mental picture, right there. Right on her needing him as badly as he needed her. No woman had ever looked at him like that. Lust, yes. Aroused, hell yeah. But need—actual life-or-death need, like he was her air, her water, her sustenance—that was a first.

Why that didn't terrify him, he had no idea.

He pushed all thought away because this night was about instinct, after all. His tongue pushed deeper and deeper while her inner muscles tried to catch it the way she'd clamped around his cock before. It might have made him laugh if he hadn't been so tuned in to the little noises she made, telling him he was the first to earn the privilege of such an intimate touch.

The first. The last. His wolf made an oath, there and then. No man would ever touch this woman again. No one but him. Just like he had no further need for any woman but her.

The idea drove him to take her higher, higher, before letting her erupt in pleasure around him.

"Kyle! Yes!" When she gasped and writhed in the grips of a mighty orgasm, his blood sang.

By the time he got her to his bed, the ache in his cock was a burn. She fell right into place under him, her legs wrapped high around his waist. He plunged home again and again, groaning out loud. She was just the right size: snug around his cock and deep as an ocean, or so it seemed. She was straining for something off the charts, something beyond the physical, and part of him was making crazy inner vows to chase down exactly what that was and bring it to her like a gift.

He glanced down, following the hard center line of her abs to the point where his cock was buried in her. He pulled back a little, just to remind himself they were two and not one. He watched, fascinated, until nothing registered but her nails on his back and the heat winding around the two of them, and they were both flying, flying, gone. He closed his eyes through the height of his pounding climax, wondering where it would end: a soft landing in a place called home, or a sudden crash into the briar patch of regret.

When he collapsed into the pillow and pulled Stef close, her body molded to his in slow, comfortable degrees. He wondered how—why—this could be. He'd gotten drunk around women. Gotten drunk with women. But never, ever had he gotten drunk on a woman—on her scent, her shape, her sensuality. The way she touched him, guided him, pleasured him... It was as if they'd been together many times before. He couldn't doubt this is how they belonged: together.

And yet he knew that night had a way of playing tricks on a man, and daylight could cast an awfully harsh spotlight on mornings-after. The next time Kyle opened his eyes, the sun was peeking over the horizon. He reached an arm out to tug Stef closer, but she was gone.

Chapter Eighteen

Stef sat on a hilltop, picking at the fraying denim of the jeans she'd slipped on before stealing out of Kyle's house. Shafts of pale yellow and pink slanted over the horizon. The colors of fear and regret. She hung her head in her arms and sniffed, but the sun prodded mercilessly, forcing her tear-streaked face up. God, what had she done? What was she becoming?

She'd slept with a man she had no right sleeping with. A friend.

A he-wolf. A shifter.

Just like you.

There it was again, that voice. The one that had pushed her to go much too far last night with a man whose touch was so soft, so secure, that she'd fallen under his spell. She'd wanted him with such desperation that it scared her, thinking only about how good it felt to be two and not one. So what if they'd been buddies fifteen years ago? Buddies didn't kiss, or lick, or hump each other like a couple of wild things in the night. Right?

It was wrong. All wrong.

Then why did it feel so right? the inner voice demanded.

The scar on her neck throbbed, and that was her answer. It was easy to believe she really felt something for Kyle, when in truth she was turning into a beast. Ron's bite must have sparked animal urges in her. Irresistible urges. What if she started spreading her legs for any male who came along at the right place and time? Worse, what if she'd come to think of it as something good? As magic—even love?

She hugged her knees tighter and hid her face again. If this was her future, she didn't want it. Crazed nights under the moon? Frantic fucks with strangers? She'd have no pride, no dignity.

Red desert rock heated under the rising sun as her cheeks burned with the memories. Of course Kyle had gone along with the impulse. He was a man, and not only a man, but a wolf—a beast that hid under the wounded warrior.

The same kind of beast that hid inside her now, too.

She wanted to be disgusted with herself, but a hot rush came with the memories. When he'd lowered her to the ground and hammered into her, she'd moaned loud enough to scratch her own throat. She hadn't just enjoyed the heat of him but gloried in it. Lovemaking like she'd never experienced—

Sex, she corrected herself. That was sex, raw and unadulterated.

Love, insisted a contralto voice she was starting to recognize as her wolf's.

Great, now she was having conversations with the beast. If that wasn't proof of her insanity, nothing was.

Her human side stomped in defiance. *I barely know him! How can it be love?*

The wolf growled. *We know him. He's ours.*

You disgust me!

The wolf snarled back. *Nothing in me didn't exist in you before. I'm part of you.*

She could have hissed. *I've never jumped a man like that before!*

The wolf snickered. *You would have if you met him. Not that boy you remember, but this man. This one!*

Stef didn't have an answer to that truth; she just got stuck there, staring at a hedgehog cactus with thorns that lined up in neat, overlapping rows. Just like her life: a hopeless maze of thorns.

The wolf countered with another rush of memories.

Friend. Lover. Mate. Hadn't he been gentle, even reverent?

She closed her eyes and remembered his thumb, sliding across her lower lip. His eyes had taken on the look of a man regarding a secret treasure, fraught with danger and reward. His arms wrapped around her like a promise to hold on forever.

Hadn't that felt good? the wolf demanded.

It did feel good. More than good. He'd given her exactly what she needed, exactly as she'd dreamed it. But that was the thing: how could something that perfect be real?

It was real. You wanted him. He wanted you. It's destiny.

She hugged herself tightly, pushing the wolf away. *I don't want him!*

Oh yes? Then why are you imagining it's his arms hugging you right now?

She jerked her arms clear of her ribs and half-jumped to her feet. Her mind raced for a reply, but her thoughts were all jumbled and her arms kept coming back to her sides, trying to squeeze away the empty ache of an emotion she didn't dare name.

Maybe last night had nothing to do with base urges and everything to do with the man. Maybe her wolf wasn't lying. She'd felt so right being with him...

Because it is right, the wolf grumbled. *We need him.*

She stiffened at the thought. She didn't need to be held, or comforted, or protected. She didn't need this man or any other. She needed... what?

She collapsed into the flimsy shelter of her own body and sucked in a long, stuttering breath. Lost, she was so lost. With nowhere to go. No one to turn to.

You have him.

She feigned deaf ears. The wolf was trying to sell her a drug she didn't want or need, but she wouldn't give in. She had to fight it, along with the attraction to him. Because somewhere inside, she was still herself, and she couldn't let that be pried out of her.

She spun around. The highway wasn't too far. She could hike out, catch a ride. Escape.

Running from yourself or from the man?

She could head south to Mexico. Wasn't that where people on the run went? She could cross the border, change her identity, and then she'd... she'd...

You'll do what?

If Kyle didn't come after her, Ron would. Ron and his pack of wolves. She could feel that in her bones. Ron's bite had forged some kind of connection that lurked in her body like a disease. Being with Kyle had kept it at bay, but sooner or later, Ron would come for her.

She shivered. Whatever danger lurked around Twin Moon Ranch, whatever weakness she had for Kyle, it was nothing like the danger posed by Ron and his North Ridge pack. Running wasn't the solution.

So stay, the wolf nodded. *Stay.*

She looked south, into the depths of the desert, then north, toward the highway, and finally east, where the peak of Kyle's roof barely showed above a rise. The pull of it was like the glow of a fire in the darkness of night. The glow of home.

Her cynical snort broke the morning silence. Running wasn't the answer, but staying had its dangers, too. Even if she could trust Kyle, she couldn't trust herself.

She'd go back, but she wouldn't cave in. She'd keep her pride, her honor. She wouldn't crumble. No matter how much she wanted to, she wouldn't crumble.

Not even for him.

Chapter Nineteen

Kyle sat on the top step of the porch, eyes fixed on the hill while his gut jumped up and down. He rubbed his eyes so hard, he saw spots. And in those spots, little highlights of an unforgettable night.

He could scent her out there, just as he could smell her regret. If only he could talk to her and explain. But he couldn't even explain what happened to himself, so what good would it be trying to tell her?

Okay, he probably—no, he definitely shouldn't have succumbed to his wolf's desire. But resisting her was like telling his lungs not to breathe or his heart not to beat. And telling himself it was wrong felt like a lie. He'd never felt that good in his life. Had never felt that full of... something warm and sweet and unfamiliar, like his veins had filled with honey and his mind floated on a pleasantly warm buzz. Because they'd had peace, real peace in those early morning hours.

His head snapped up at a movement in the distance. Stef was coming out of the hills. She came striding along like an Amazon, so tough and bristling, he could almost hear her armor clink. He pulled in a slow breath and let it out again, counting the seconds until she came thumping up the stairs as if she was planning to sweep right past him and fly into the house.

Well, he wasn't letting her fly anywhere, not yet. Not like this.

He parked himself on the top step, right in her path.

Stomp, stomp, stop. She came to a thudding halt, one step below.

"Stef," he started, not really sure what he'd say next.

101

She glared.

Yeah, she was upset. He got the message. But it was a stubborn, forced kind of glare. The kind that said she was trying to convince herself as much as him.

"Look," they both said at exactly the same time.

For a minute, she glared on, but then the anger seeped away and all he saw before she dropped her eyes was pain. Pain and emptiness. He would have bartered anything for the right word or gesture to make things right, but the desert wasn't exactly throwing ideas at him, not the way it had been wildly suggesting last night.

"Stef," he tried again, trying to make it softer this time. A plea, not an accusation. "What's wrong?"

She tilted her head up slowly, and it was awkward, standing on the steps like that. But she seemed okay with awkward, so he didn't move. Her jaw was clenching, and a vein on her neck pulsed.

"Everything's wrong," she mumbled. Her hands fluttered in the air as she searched for words.

"Last night wasn't wrong." He meant for it to come out soft, but it was more of a declaration. The second part, though, came out in a whisper. "Us, I mean. You didn't want it?"

His ears strained for her answer.

"I wanted it too much," she whispered.

He could barely hear her voice after her chin dropped and her shoulders rounded like a turtle halfway into its shell. God, he wished he could see something other than the top of her head. He put a finger under her chin and tipped it up so he could see the warm brown of her eyes, sparking gold and green. Scared and defiant at the same time. Shining with tears she refused to release.

"I barely know you," she said.

"You know me," he growled.

"We were kids then..."

"What's so different now?"

She looked away and let a finger wander to the scar on her neck. "A lot of things."

He shook his head and looked at her long and hard until she was forced to look back.

"So okay, we grew up."

She snorted. "Sure did."

"But what's so different?" No one had ever understood him as well as her; no one ever would.

She opened her mouth with a retort, but then closed it again, along with her glistening eyes. Slowly, she leaned forward until her forehead was on his chest and let his arms slide around her shoulders to pull her close. And even though it hurt to see her so upset, something in him sang.

She wanted it too much. She wanted him.

"I'm just so...so mixed-up," she sniffed into the fabric of his shirt.

He snorted. "If I'd been half as together as you the morning after my first change..."

Part of him wanted to sit her in his kitchen and feed her cookies and warm milk; the other part wanted to take her to his bedroom and have her again and again. It was just like last night, when his the wolf had chanted for him to bite her—on their first night! The beast was no better than Ron, getting carried away on the intense scent of a Changeling. Damn wolf was getting greedy.

Damn wolf knows his mate when he scents her, came the rumbling reply.

He pulled her up to the top step and hugged her long and close, scrunching his eyes tightly like that might keep reality away. If only it could be him and her and nothing else.

"Some things don't change, Stef."

"Yeah?" She sniffed, but there was a tiny thread of hope in it. "Like what?"

"Like what really counts." *Like you and me and someday,* he wanted to add, but couldn't quite get that part out. "Like us."

His voice wavered, and his wolf barked inside. *Get yourself together, man!*

How many times had he said just that during the days that followed his first shift, five years ago? He'd woken up shivering on the floor of his old apartment, covered in dried blood and vaguely aware that not all of it was his own. The kitchen looked like a sledgehammer had gone to work on it—that or a wild animal, crazed and caged. Wallpaper hung in great shreds, fluttering in the breeze stealing in from a shattered window. He'd stalked back there after his wolf had tired of its first rampage. Was it a deer he had torn apart in the madness of that first shift, or a man?

He'd made for the open road after that, leaving his job and his home and the couple of acquaintances he sometimes called friends, and tried drinking the wolf out of his system for a time. Nearly had the animal drowned in alcohol when Tina found him slumped in a back alley and leaned over him with a quiet tsk, tsk. *What are we going to do with you, wolf?*

He had no such question now, though. He knew exactly what he wanted to do with this she-wolf. Like keep her safe. Keep her close. Make her his.

Another minute spent wrapped around her and he might just give in to that urge. But she was shoving away from him again, and the regret was back.

"Look," she said in a shaky voice. "I don't even know what I want." She tried a little smile. "Except maybe a shower."

He could read the subtext in the way she hugged her arms to herself. *I need time, space.*

Their eyes met, and he felt the longing as clearly as the confusion raging inside her. Then her jaw clicked, and she hurried past. A second later, the screen door banged shut.

He sat down on the top step. Hard.

His wolf was pacing inside. *Maybe she doesn't know about destined mates. Maybe we should tell her. Maybe—*

Maybe she doesn't feel it, too, he snapped right back.

A minute later, he heard the shower running. He pressed his palms to the hollows of his eyes, and he told himself he should be grateful that she'd come back at all. And if his lower ribs were aching, well, he'd just call that regret.

She hid in the shower for a long time. The sound of trickling water reached out to him through the walls, and every strand of muscle in his body strained as his wolf contemplated bursting in and stopping her from erasing his scent.

If only he could sit her down and explain to her.

So explain! his wolf cried.

Right, how would that go? *Stef, there's a lot of good about the shifter life.*

Yeah, that would go over well. She'd been dragged kicking and screaming into this world. A little like him.

It's true, he'd try to explain. *There's a lot that's good. Really good.* But he'd never been that talented with words, and how could he explain? The feeling of being one with the natural world. The old-fashioned honesty of the Twin Moon Ranch folk. The sense of community.

She could relate to all of that, right? She'd probably thrive on it. There were a number of young women she could relate to, too, given the chance: Rae, Lana, Heather—especially Heather, who'd been turned too, albeit of her own free will.

Which was the crux of the problem. Stef hadn't come seeking any of this. She certainly hadn't come seeking a reunion or an unbridled night of sex. And even if he hadn't pushed her too far by stepping over that line, he knew he was hardly a shining star of integration. He lived out on the fringes, as he'd always done.

Your own damn choice, his wolf grumbled. *We belong in the pack. Really in the pack.*

In truth, he wasn't sure where he belonged. Not human, not wolf. Somewhere in between. Always somewhere in between. As an officer of the law, that went without saying. As a kid, it had been the same. He was an outsider and always had been. Becoming half wolf hadn't changed a thing.

She can change things.

He shook his head. A man like him would always be alone. It was the way it was.

He picked himself off the step and forced himself to brew a cup of coffee. Decaf. God knows his system didn't need any more stimulation, not on a morning like this. Then he walked around the back of the house to the woodpile, itching for something to bend, break, or shatter. But even when he had the ax in his hand and the first piece of wood balanced on a stump, ready to split, the words echoed in his mind.

Alone. Always alone.

He glared at the wood, weighed the ax in his hands before swinging his shoulders up, then hammered down with everything he had.

Bang!

The wood split almost to its base. A twist of the ax finished the rest, and the halves fell to the ground. Again and again, he raised the ax; again and again, he pounded it down. The next time he took stock, he was standing in a pile of wood chips with sweat pouring down his brow. Did he feel better?

He made a face then pulled another dozen logs over and started again. He would have been at it for another hour if it hadn't been for the phone ringing, demanding he come inside.

It was Tina, calling him in to another meeting.

"Bring Stefanie," she said, and her voice was grim.

Chapter Twenty

Kyle gripped the steering wheel harder with every passing minute of the drive. Stefanie sat beside him in the passenger seat with her arms firmly folded, scrutinizing the scenery.

If he could just manage to break past the lump in his throat, he'd tell her to give up looking for some truth out there. There was no such thing as destiny. No hope. Just patches of dirt, thorns, and scrub. Life was as bleak as the desert, and she might as well get used to it. He'd long since resigned himself to the realities of life.

Except these last days with her. Little bits of happiness had come filtering into his corner of the desert since she'd appeared. Tiny pleasures, like the sight of two coffee cups in the sink and not just one. Hearing the floorboards creak under someone else's step as the house came to life with her presence, her scent. The scent that had wrapped around him last night and led him down the road to pleasure and peace.

A peace that was shattered the minute the truck rattled over the last cattle grid and under the ranch gate. The leaves of the mighty cottonwoods that towered over the ranch grounds might have been dancing a happy jig, but even that couldn't smother the sense of foreboding in the air. Tina hadn't said what the meeting was about, but one glance at two unfamiliar pickups in the lot—pickups with Colorado plates—and Kyle knew.

"Stef—"

But before he could grab Stefanie and get her away from this place, far and fast, she was out of the car and climbing the steps to the council house with the raised chin of a noblewoman on her way to the guillotine.

"Wait—"

He nearly ran into her at the threshold, where she'd stopped in midstep. He could hear the catch in her breath, see her face drain of color as she looked inside.

It wasn't the sight of Ty, eyes aflame with alpha power that did it, nor that of Tina, mouth set hard. Nor was it the rare sight of Cody bristling in anger. It was the two shadowy figures on the right.

The sloppy one with greedy, restless eyes could only be Ron. A tiny corner of tongue darted out from between cracked lips and let out a swipe at the sight of Stefanie. Even from a distance, he reeked of stale cigarettes. He stood slightly hunched, like a vulture waiting for the lion to take down his intended prey.

The lion being the North Ridge alpha, Greer, who towered above everyone but Ty. A hulk of a man, Greer barely hid his inner wolf. It was grinning in the points of his teeth, tangled in the hairy mats of his arms, huffing with each heavy breath. Kyle knew the brute by reputation: a merciless fighter, a hard-ruling alpha, a man used to getting what he wanted.

Greer's eyes undressed Stefanie then slid over to Ron. Kyle didn't need to hear his thoughts to catch the gist of the silent message passing between the two men.

She's just as you said. Greer nodded in approval. *I'll have to try her myself.*

Ron scowled but flicked his eyes down in submission. *As you wish.*

He had heard of such things—of alphas who took of their own pack's mates as they desired. Some called it a Tribute, others, Alpha's Choice. It was rare, it was barbarian, but it still happened, at least in some packs. Packs like North Ridge.

His wolf started snarling as the implications of it all sank in. Another bite would bind Stefanie to Ron—and by extension, to Greer. She'd stay with Ron and endure, a slave to their forced bond. Kyle had responded to enough domestic abuse calls to guess what Stefanie would become. She'd get that haunted, hollow look that all battered women got. That spark, that spunk that defined his brown-eyed girl would be extinguished.

Over my dead body, his wolf declared, coiling for attack.

He was about to leap when a flash that was all Stefanie whipped right up to Ron and let a fist fly. He heard the sharp whack before he registered what was happening. No sissy slap, that one, but a full-on uppercut that knocked Ron back on his heels. She was winding up for another punch when Kyle dragged her back.

Not now, my mate, his wolf tried telling her, but she didn't seem to hear.

Greer pulled Ron away with a show of mock outrage, and Kyle couldn't help but hiss in the alpha's face. Greer went rock hard, his eyes boring into Kyle, demanding he submit. But Kyle was no beta, not in his pack, not in Greer's, and there was more on the line than his own pride. He held the alpha's gaze, meeting the challenge.

Over my dead body, his wolf snarled back at Greer.

That can be arranged. Greer scowled right back.

Try me, asshole.

It is wasn't for Ty socking him with a look that ordered him to back down, he'd have attacked.

Stef remained coiled at his side, her eyes throwing daggers.

"Ron." She all but spit the name out. "How's your nose?"

Now that she mentioned it, Kyle could see the bend in the vulture's beak. The one she must have put there when she fought him off.

"How's your neck?" Ron sneered back.

"Come a little closer and I'll show you."

Yeah, asshole. One step closer.

Ron didn't take the bait, of course. He was the type who eschewed boldness, a man who waited for others to drop their guard. A dangerous foe, in his own dirty way. Kyle was ready to shove the weasel toward the door when Ty let out a low growl that stopped everyone in their tracks. A moment later, Cody's smooth voice was getting things under control again.

"So," the co-alpha started. His tone was light, but the bulging sinews of his throat gave away the facade. "Let's try this again." He shot Stefanie a bolstering look, and for all the rage glowing in Kyle's body, he felt lucky for the thousandth time to have ended up in Twin Moon pack. Together, Cody and Ty formed the perfect leadership team: tough and uncompromising on one hand, diplomatic and supportive on the other.

Greer spoke up, his voice as rough-hewn as a mountain mine. "We're here to finish what we started."

"The hell you will," Kyle growled, stepping in front of Stefanie.

"What you started?" Stef shot back. "As if anyone gave you the right!"

"Don't think the lady's interested," Cody said, his voice sanding away the tension in the room.

"She has no choice," Greer snapped.

"Of course she has a choice," Kyle all but shouted.

"Every woman has a choice," Tina insisted.

"You know the law." Greer addressed Ty with a look that said women should be seen and not heard. Ron was sneering in the background, fingers twitching as he took in his would-be prize.

"Law?" Stefanie asked, incredulous. "Don't get me started on the law."

Kyle put a hand on her arm, trying to calm her down. If only he'd had the time to explain that there were human laws and there were shifter laws.

"A wolf bitten is a wolf claimed," Cody said.

Kyle glared. What was Cody doing, strengthening their enemy's case?

Greer and Ron nodded smugly, but Cody put his hands up quickly. "But not a human and not half-bit." He shot Ron a look that said, *Such a pity you didn't get it right.* Then he turned up his palms. *Boys, you got a problem. Not our problem; yours.*

"She's ours!" Greer snarled.

She's mine! his wolf howled inside.

"I'm nobody's!" Stefanie shouted, giving Greer the evil eye.

Defiant as her words were, Kyle sensed the sadness behind them. She had no one. Just like him.

Cody gave Ty a nod; the brothers were in agreement about something.

"She goes nowhere," Ty said with finality that dared anyone to suggest otherwise. "We'll consult with the elders of three packs—ours, yours, and a neutral pack's. Then we'll see. In the meantime, she stays put."

She stays put, his wolf echoed.

Greer opened his mouth as if to protest then closed it upon seeing the flames in Ty's eyes. "Two days," he grumbled and stalked out of the room with Ron skulking at his heels. "I give you two days."

We give you nothing, Kyle let his whole body say.

Stefanie held her haughty stance until the two men were out the door then let her shoulders fold. Kyle caught her arm just as she reached out for balance and ran a calming hand over her back. To hell with what the others thought. A rush went through him when she didn't shrug him off but leaned in.

The moment his fingers made contact with her, his wolf reared up inside, bugling like an elk. *Mine! Mate!*

The world narrowed to only him and her and the electric tingling passing between them at the point of contact.

Mate. The feeling was so strong, he couldn't deny it, but he couldn't quite believe it, either. A mate, for him, the lone wolf?

Cody brushed past on his way to the door then froze and slowly rotated to face him. The co-alpha sniffed the air, his eyebrows pulled tight. When Cody leaned closer, his eyes darted between Kyle and Stefanie, then went wide.

Kyle felt his stomach sink. *Oh, shit.*

The thin hope that had just been reborn crashed and burned as Cody hauled him toward the door.

"Her scent is all over you, man," the co-alpha whispered, throwing a glance back at Stefanie. "Jesus, what were you thinking?"

Kyle felt the heat rise in his face, cursing himself for not thinking of that before. He'd cleaned up before coming over, but he hadn't exactly scrubbed. Not that that would have

111

masked the fresh scent of sex; wolf noses were too keen. A good thing he hadn't come any closer to Greer.

He forced his gaze level with Cody's, even though his eyes burned from the contact. Saying *it just happened* really wouldn't cut it, but neither was he letting anyone—not even the pack leadership—question him about Stef.

"Don't," he warned Cody.

"You were supposed to be keeping her safe, not making things worse," Cody hissed, pulling him outside.

I am keeping her safe, his wolf grumbled. *I will always keep her safe.*

Kyle yanked his arm back but followed Cody, if only to spare Stefanie extra attention. That, and he'd prefer fewer witnesses to his own shame. He'd never, ever compromised his pack before. Unclaimed females were fair game, but Stefanie had been marked by a member of the North Ridge pack. Strictly speaking, she was off-limits. Way, way off-limits.

Now his pack wasn't just out on a limb, it was dangling over a sheer cliff. Because in the shifter world, touching a female claimed by another pack was akin to a declaration of war—and North Ridge had a reputation for fighting first and asking questions later.

"Jesus, do you know what you've done?" Cody blurted once they were outside.

"Nothing that wasn't right."

Kyle almost did a double take when he realized it wasn't the wolf speaking, but his heart. There'd been so much in his life that wasn't right, yet Stef stood out from the rest like a sunflower among dandelions. He didn't understand why or how, but being with her was right.

He took a deep breath and looked Cody straight in the eye. He'd done the pack wrong, and he would face what he must. But there was another side to the equation, and he had to set the record straight.

"Tell me you'd let an innocent woman get claimed by North Ridge. Tell me you're willing to stand by and do nothing."

"No, I don't want to see her get claimed by North Ridge. But we have to consider our pack first, and she's not one of ours."

"She could be."

If Cody was taken aback, Kyle was downright shocked at his own words. Had he really just said that?

Cody's expression went from anger to wonder. "You mean it."

He gulped but kept his eyes steady. "Yes, I meant it."

Cody leaned in. "You love her."

Kyle didn't move his lips, but he didn't have to. His whole body screamed *Yes.*

Cody studied him from head to toe for any trace of a lie. Then—Kyle couldn't believe it—Cody cracked into a smile: a secret smile that seemed to arise from some private memory.

"Well, then, I guess you'd better do what you have to do."

Tina and Stefanie came out of the council room, and Cody leaned in toward Kyle with a harsh whisper. "Just watch you don't fuck things up."

Chapter Twenty-One

Stefanie tried tuning everything out, from the rattle of the tires to the pounding of her heart, but it wasn't working. Looking outside the window as Kyle drove down the back road did no good; the Arizona landscape was so big, it threatened to swallow her up. Those few minutes of barely controlled rage in the council house had cost her dearly. Now she was hunched and trembling, a complete mess. And even though Kyle's hand was tight over hers, promising that every minute was a mile farther from the enemy, she couldn't escape the truth.

Ron had come for her.

She thought that was as bad as it could get, except it was worse. There was Greer. The way the man's eyes traveled up and down her body told her all too well what he had in mind.

It was bad enough to be on the run from a lunatic. But it was worse: the lunatic wasn't a man, but a werewolf. And now there were two werewolves after her—and Greer was a far greater threat than Ron. How had she ever gotten herself into this mess? She used to have a normal life. A job. A home.

The pickup rattled along in quiet challenge. What exactly was normal? She didn't know any more. And as for having a life, well. . . she'd been doing a lot of wishing even before all this happened to her. Wishing for a little more balance. Wishing she weren't quite so alone.

We're not alone. We have the pack, her wolf said.

Right, she snorted back. *North Ridge pack can't wait for me to join.*

The wolf let out an inner growl so sharp, so angry, she flinched.

This pack. Twin Moon. We belong here.

115

Stefanie wanted to slap the inner voice away and insist she didn't belong anywhere, but denial wouldn't help. She had to understand. She took a deep breath, hoping Kyle was ready for the tough questions. Hoping she was ready to face the answers.

"So what happens now?"

He lifted an eyebrow the way a dog lifts an ear, and the effect had a certain charm. "We wait."

"Wait for what? For someone else to decide what's best for me? Wait to be handed over to North Ridge?" She choked on the words.

She buried her face in her hands, an ostrich with its head in the sand, until Kyle's voice coaxed her out. "Stef," he said softly, and for a moment, she wished everything in the world would go away. Everything but him.

"Stef."

She looked up in spite of herself and found his gaze terrifyingly determined. "I will never let you go." His voice ground over the words, like they'd been mined from the deepest part of his soul. A ripple went through his shoulders, as if to say *There, I said it. I mean it, and I will hold to my words.* His whole body went into a stiff military stance. *They will take you over my dead body.*

Something inside Stef tingled as she soaked in the promise coursing through his hand, closed over hers. Just for now, she decided to believe that this would somehow turn out all right. Kyle Williams, neighborhood bad boy and Arizona law enforcement officer, said so.

She wasn't alone. Not any more.

She lost herself in the warmth of his hand, the scent of him. There was more of it here in the car than in his house, as if he felt more at home on the road. As if the two of them could drive and drive and find some escape in the hills.

But neither Kyle nor the car could shield her from her other enemy: the moon. She could feel it lurking beyond the horizon, waiting for its chance to climb high in the sky and claim her again.

Her hands twisted her seat belt. "Is it going to happen again tonight?"

Kyle shot her a sharp glance, and heat rushed through her face as she realized the innuendo. The moon bringing out her wolf wasn't the only momentous event of the previous night. She cleared her throat. "I mean, am I going to...to change? Moon's still full, right?"

Kyle shifted in his seat. "Close to full."

"So? Am I going to change?"

His thought process took a lot longer than his answer. "Maybe."

"Are you going to change?"

His head swayed ever so slightly, weighing things up. "Possibly."

Stefanie threw her hands up with a frustrated huff.

Kyle made a grating noise. "Definitely."

"Why? Because the moon makes you?" Now that her tongue had gotten warmed up, the words were cascading out. She was tired of mysteries and half-truths.

Kyle shook his head. "The moon is only part of it. It affects humans, too, you know."

She gave him her best army stare: *Don't change the subject, Williams.*

He sighed. "We can shift any time. Not just at night. Not just at full moon."

Shift, she told herself, slowly growing accustomed to the vocabulary of this foreign language.

"I don't get why anyone would want to shift at all."

Part of her wished he'd turn those blue eyes toward her when he spoke. They made everything brighter, more hopeful.

"It's part of you, Stef. The wolf is always there, inside. You can't keep it caged."

Deep inside, she heard a canine grunt of agreement.

"The wolf has to come out," he went on. "It feels good to let him run free."

Free. That part sounded good. What she wouldn't give to be free of this crazy shifter world.

"So, yes, tonight I will shift. It helps."

She couldn't help but cock her head at that. "Helps with what?"

He clamped his lips together like he'd just let a secret slip. "It just...helps."

Stef wondered what he needed help with. Stress? Anger? Loneliness?

She glanced at his face, but it was set in a carefully neutral expression just as it had been, way back when. Maybe the ghosts that haunted him as a kid had never quite slipped away. Hers rattled their chains in her mental attic all the time, so why would his be any different?

Her thigh twitched, and she remembered the pain of the shift.

"Will it hurt again?" she whispered, and damn it, her voice cracked.

His Adam's apple bobbed, and he paused before carefully packaging his words. "It doesn't hurt, not after the first couple of times. There's even kind of a...high that goes with it."

"Right. A high," she mumbled. She let her eyes slide shut, trying not to imagine shifting again. What kind of crazy rampage was a wolf capable of? What if she couldn't change back? What if—

Something nudged her side, and she glanced down to find Kyle's hand seeking out hers again. His eyes were still on the road, his jaw locked hard, but his touch was gentle. She let her eyes close again as her fingers slowly welcomed his.

"Kyle," she whispered and sensed him nod for her to go on. "How did it happen to you? Becoming a...shifter?"

His fingers went tense, and even with the noise of the truck, she could hear him pull in a long, slow breath of air.

"A biker fight," he said at last, exactly as a bush screeched along the length of the truck. "We were called in to break it up." She peeked and saw that his knuckles had gone bone white over the gear stick. He let the truck hammer over a series of scalloped ruts in the road before continuing. "Got dragged into it. One guy was going nuts, fighting wild. At the time, we figured he was high..." He trailed off, shaking his head slightly. "Turns out he wasn't human but a rogue."

Rogue?

"A rogue wolf. An outcast." Kyle's voice was bitter.

She let a couple of heartbeats pound by. "Did they get him?"

He shook his head—no—and Stefanie pushed deep into her seat, trying to escape the injustices of the world. "And that's enough to change a person? Into a wolf?" she asked.

A muscle in Kyle's jaw twitched. "Usually not."

She looked at him, willing him to go on.

"Usually, you die." The shrug of his shoulders belied the weight of his words. "It's rare to survive. Or so I'm told."

The knife of fear sliced through her even though she knew he'd survived. She'd lost too many people she loved already.

Love? The word echoed in her mind.

Love, the inner voice growled.

"But you didn't die," she croaked over the lump in her throat.

Kyle's brow tightened, and the eyebrows pulled taut as a tightly drawn bow. "No." His tone was almost disappointed, and her heart cried out. Before she could respond, he caught her hand and squeezed it. "Neither did you."

Love. Her wolf purred.

Stef straightened in her seat, trying to ignore the voice and the warm something coursing through her veins. No, she hadn't died from her neck wound—but she was far from being in the clear. She let her fingers run absently along the ridges of muscle in his arm, unwilling to break the contact.

"Are there others? On the ranch, I mean?"

"Other wolves who were turned?"

She nodded, catching hold of the word and adding it to her vocabulary list. *Turned.*

Kyle's chin dipped. "Just one at Twin Moon. Heather—Cody's mate."

Mate. That word was already on the list. High up, in bold.

"But Heather was different," Kyle added. "She only came after she and Cody...after..."

She studied his profile. "After they fell in love?"

Kyle gave her a curt military nod, and she had to wonder at him. Was the word so hard for him to say? Then she remembered some of the sounds that used to come from his house, way back from when they were neighbors. The shouts, the slammed doors, the cries. Then it was her turn to tighten her jaw and clam up. Maybe love wasn't a word that fell as easily from some people's lips as from others.

Those very kissable lips. Her wolf sighed.

"What?" Kyle asked, catching her expression.

"Nothing," she murmured and let her eyelids seal the sight of him away.

Chapter Twenty-Two

The rest of the drive went by in a turbulent kind of silence as Stefanie seesawed back on her emotions. The minute they got to the house, Kyle stalked around to the woodpile out back and went straight back to chopping. If she'd had her running shoes or mountain bike handy, she would have set out on her own therapy session: pounding the pedals, breathing in the clean air, reveling in the space. There was something magical about this part of the West, that was for sure.

But she didn't have the bike, nor the means to escape the angry sound of splintering wood coming from the back of the house. She finally gave in to the urge and rose from where she'd been sitting on the front step, her joints creaking. Would shifting eventually render her crippled? Her body was somewhere between horribly sore and nicely stretched right now. The people on the ranch—the shapeshifters, she corrected herself—seemed sprightly enough, though. More than sprightly, in fact. They were downright athletic, men and women alike. The thought stayed with her as she followed the sounds of chopping around the back. Everyone she'd seen at the ranch seemed supremely healthy. Happy.

Buff.

The word popped into her mind as she came around the corner and spotted Kyle hefting an ax. Shirtless. Sweaty. And wow: buff. There wasn't another word for muscles stacked like bricks, one on top of the other along the line of his abdomen. The steely cords that ran from his shoulders down his arms looked like the support structure of a bridge, and the flat plates of his pecs glistened under the sun. All of it just this side of intimidating.

121

Just.

"You keep a fire burning all winter here?" she asked him.

He just looked at her, a bead of sweat running down his jaw.

"I mean, it's Arizona, not Alaska." She went for a light tone because that might hide the triple-speed pumping of her heart.

One side of his mouth crooked, like he was trying to remember how to smile. "We're at high altitude here. It gets cold."

"Cold? In Arizona?"

He shrugged. "Well, kind of cold."

She laughed, and that felt good. "You turning into a softie, Williams?"

He stood there, legs shoulder width apart, gripping the ax with one hand at the base and one near the head. There was nothing soft about him, except maybe that look in his eye.

"Watch it, Alt."

She smiled at the use of her last name; military talk. And just like that, they were back to being the buddies they'd once been. Or an extension of the buddies, now all grown up.

"Need help?" she asked as goose bumps erupted along her skin.

The man could be standing beside a giant sequoia with a Swiss Army knife and he wouldn't need help, but she had to say something.

"Sure."

She followed the tilt of his head to where a second ax leaned against a shed. Taking it in her hands, she measured the balance of it before reaching for a piece of wood and standing it on a stump not far from Kyle's. She backed away, concentrating on her target.

Imagine Ron, her wolf murmured.

Stefanie swung the ax high and let it rip.

Wham!

The wood gave a mighty crack and yielded under the blade, and she imagined lightning, striking Ron down.

"You're gonna chop your way right to China if you keep that up," Kyle warned.

"Stuff it, Williams."

He chuckled and the sound warmed her soul.

Grinning at her own handiwork, she swung again. Soon, she was lost in the affirming rush of it all, the mirage of power. Every stroke, every solid thunk helped ease the helplessness away. Maybe she'd have some say in her fate, after all.

Kyle watched a while longer then went back to his own chopping, and both of them let their axes do the talking. The windmill squeaked as it turned in slow circles, lending a steady rhythm to the staccato notes of their work. Gradually, sweat and the slanting light of afternoon rubbed a kind of rosy balm over her bitter mood, loosening her mind just enough to pursue other thoughts. Dangerous thoughts, like how nice it would be to live a quiet life at the edge of the desert with a quiet man who spoke with his eyes and his actions. A place under the boundless Arizona sky, where things seemed simpler.

She stopped chopping long enough to study her hands. Blisters were forming at the creases of her palms, but even as she rubbed them, the sting eased.

A shadow fell over her as Kyle took one of her hands and studied it closely. His fingers were sure and strong, like knotted branches of bristlecone pine, and the warmth radiating from them went straight to her gut. She nearly hummed, the contact felt so good.

"Is it normal to heal this fast?" she whispered, reluctant to disturb the peace that had settled over both of them.

Even with the sweat—or maybe because of it—he smelled good. Sinfully good.

"All shifters do that." He nodded, thumbs massaging her palms.

Shifters. She was one now, too.

She looked at her hands cupped in his and tried to memorize the sight and the feel of him there. He was only a couple of inches taller, but his hands dwarfed hers. Like the rest of him, they were solid and steady. Honest.

"Then what about getting old?"

He pulled her hands upward and clasped them in his. God, those eyes were blue. Bluer than the sky.

"Shifters live longer than regular humans."

She gave in to the temptation to curl her fingers around his. "Like how long?"

"Depends. Two hundred and fifty, maybe three hundred years. Some even longer."

"A long time," she murmured, feeling suddenly weary. Three centuries was a long time to be alone. Unless. . .

She stood close to him, wondering what exactly she had lost when she left Colorado and what she might have found here in Arizona. Her eyes traveled along the natural curve of the land over Kyle's shoulder. Maybe the answer was hidden in the contours of the little hollow where his house stood. Or beyond, in that vast vista, beige and brown and scrubby but undeniably alive. The desert was a place where time and space took on new definition.

A thrush called from somewhere in the brush, leaves rustled in the breeze, and a familiar hum started coursing through her bones.

Home. The word formed in her mind, cued by the desert.

Home? The skeptical part of her protested just as Kyle pulled away from her, scrubbing a hand through his hair and looking suddenly confused.

Home, her wolf persisted.

She stood stock-still, hardly breathing. Was there really was such a place?

Probably not, she concluded as Kyle beat a quick retreat around the corner of the house.

She watched him go, blinking, while her stomach fluttered inside.

Don't let him go, instinct said. *Never let him go.*

Acting on their own, her feet carried her around the house, then up the stairs. Kyle stood on the far side of the porch, over by the lonely chair that faced east. His back was turned to her, his shoulders stooped, his chin bent to his chest. She could see both his hands gripping the railing as if the world was spinning and he was afraid to be thrown into space. Did he hear the urging, too?

She told herself to sweep straight into the house. Her hands—she ought to wash her hands then retreat to her room and pretend this humming sensation about to engulf her didn't exist.

Hands. Wash hands.

If her mind was a chorus of a hundred, a couple of aging sopranos would be croaking out that line. The other ninety-eight voices, however, were chanting *Home, home, home.* An entire section of basses held the word, stretching it out in her mind. Over them was the sure sound of tenors and altos, singing at a faster clip. Tempting, pleading, nodding Kyle's way.

Home, home, home.

Hands. Wash hands, squeaked the minority.

Home. Home. Home, the rest roared.

It was no contest, and she knew it.

Chapter Twenty-Three

She walked over, obeying the invisible force that reeled her in. When Kyle pushed himself away from the banister and turned, a bead of sweat glinted on his furrowed brow. Whatever it was that was happening to her, he felt it, too.

She walked right up to him. Close. Kissing-close.

"I can't do this any more, Kyle." she whispered.

"Do what?"

"Fight this."

His mouth cracked open and though no sound came, words were spilling from his eyes. Words like *shouldn't* and *can't* and *not allowed.* His eyes, though, were flickering with need so intense, it made her lungs press against her ribs. Even then, words continued to pour from her inner chorus.

Words like *friend.* She stepped closer.

Home. Her hands slid up his arms and around his neck, pulling herself into the expanse of his bare chest.

Mate. She knotted herself firmly around his frame and brought her lips to his.

Her wolf hummed as the kiss went deeper. Every nerve ending in her body zinged as she held on, tight as a cowboy in a rodeo. Home had never felt so warm, so strong, so near. Home never felt this sure or this sincere.

By the third or four thump of her heart, she could exhale. Because if a solid block of muscle and masculine flesh could melt slowly into a sappy goo, well, then it must mean something other than *No, thanks.* Something more like *Yes. Please. Be mine.*

Home had never been such a perfect fit, from the moist line of his lips right down to the hook of her calf behind his. She released a sigh and let her fingers go from death grip to a tour of inspection, wanting to feel every curve and bend of his body. There were a lot of them to study, especially on his back, where the layered muscles slid and heated under her touch.

"Stef," Kyle whispered. His voice was hoarse, like he'd been screaming at himself to resist. "We shouldn't."

She shook her head, dragging his lips with hers to work in the refusal. "Shouldn't," she said, lifting her lips just long enough to hurry the words out, "isn't an option." She deepened the kiss, opening her mouth and slowly, subtly, shaped the word *Home* into his lips.

His whole body quivered, and she marveled at his resolve. She could feel his need as clearly as she felt the bonds holding him back.

She let her fingers trail down his chest. "I can't not have you." The words came with a conviction that startled her.

"It's complicated," he tried. His hands, though, were moving up and down her back, refusing to let go.

She nudged her hips closer. "Not right now, it's not." She was nosing his ear now. "There's only you," she whispered, pulling one of his hands into hers. "And me," she finished, bringing it to her breast.

A strangled sound came from his mouth as she leaned into another kiss. "The pack. . ." he murmured, then trailed off.

She almost wished he was wearing a shirt so she could grab the collar and shake the last bit of resistance out of him. "This isn't about the pack, Kyle." Her voice cracked, and she gave up on words completely, letting her eyes have a try. The man was like a marine: *Semper Fi* was tattooed onto his soul, and Twin Moon pack was his Stars and Stripes. But didn't he know that duty didn't preclude love? She nearly said it out loud. Duty wasn't everything in life. Not by a long shot. Because what meaning did duty have if it wasn't backed by love?

She brought her thumbs gently under both sides of his jaw and stroked from his neck out to the chin and back. The prickle of his stubble was like the striking surface of a matchbox, setting off another flare of carnal need.

"You think this will only make things worse?" she asked, and it was almost a dare.

He nodded slowly, though his pulse hammered and the angle of his lips cried for more.

"Then I want worse," she said.

The flicker in his eyes flared, and then his lips caught hers in a kiss that had her whole body melting into his. As his tongue slid across hers, her free fall became a soaring climb into space. His hands tightened around her waist, and when a sigh escaped his lips, she knew she wasn't the only one rocketing away on this crazy flight.

The kiss went on and on as she pressed into him. Whatever mess they might get themselves into, it would be worth it if she could stay this close. She let her hands explore his back, her pulse skipping at every bump in that heated terrain. Her hips started to rock with little nudges that grew more insistent with every quick breath. Kyle's hands slid down her back, and then lower, tugging her good and close and fluttering every one of her nerves.

"Mmmm," she mumbled over the hum in her ears. Was that her wolf purring or his? "I'm thinking maybe this was meant to be."

"This?" he whispered, lips barely leaving her neck.

"This." She wrapped her leg around his, pushing her hips to his groin.

His hands slid even lower, and the solid comfort of them had her imagining a hundred unrushed mornings waking up beside this man. Naked, sated, close. A lifetime of mornings—that's what she wanted. To know that this wasn't just tonight, but forever. There'd be no more spinning like a compass without a north.

"Take this off," he urged, tugging at the hem of her shirt.

She smiled into his lips. "But it's my favorite shirt." The yellow one he'd given her.

"You'll get it back." He drew his hands up, and the shirt came with them. "Later. Much later."

The cool slide of fabric over her skin was replaced by the heated touch of his work-hardened hands—quick, clever hands that had her bra off like it was never there. Like there'd never been any barriers between them.

"Later. . ." she mumbled, struggling to follow her own train of thought. Action was easier, like stretching her shoulders up and back, ready to cede him everything. Because all she wanted was him, any way he liked as long as it was now. His fingers spread wide, teasing her breasts, and a thousand brush fires roared through her nerves. Hands that big and tough and strong would be capable of holding the two of them together if fate tried to pry them apart.

"Maybe," he murmured, running his lips along her jaw.

Her skin tingled under the delicious scrape of his stubble, and a shiver of anticipation zinged right down to her core.

"Maybe this was meant to be?" She wanted to sound disappointed, but that was hard with every sensor in her body bouncing off the charts.

"Probably." He was teasing her now, with his words and with his fingers. They closed over her breasts and stroked.

"Probably?" she squeaked, arching her back as her nipples stood at attention. Something about his touch made her feel bigger, fuller. Prouder, almost.

"Definitely," Kyle said, dipping to let his lips close over her aching bud.

Need speared through her body as she fisted her hands in his hair. When she moaned and ground her hips against his rigid cock, his lips curled in a smile. Home became a place to latch on to, to wind her legs around.

"Definitely meant to be," he murmured.

His arms closed around her and lifted, and the bob of his sure step told her he was carrying her inside. Her bones were mush, her blood pounding as the screen door creaked and the bright light of day grew muted. Kyle's weight shifted as he pushed the door to his room open with a foot then lowered her slowly to the bed in a dreamy journey that had her heart singing. In just a few steps, the man had taken her far away from trouble and into a soft, safe place. A place where two lovers could give and take and give all over again.

Vaguely, she wondered if love could really move so fast. But maybe this wasn't as fast as it seemed. Maybe it was slow— something years in the making, until two souls separated could once again unite.

"Gotta get rid of these." His fingers ran along the edge of her shorts.

Her body danced under his searing touch, wiggling as she stripped eagerly out of her remaining clothing.

"And these." She bit her lip as she dipped into the waistband of his jeans then eased the zipper down. "Definitely need to get rid of these."

He jerked under her touch, and she bit back a smile. Greed took over and she pushed down his clothes, letting his cock spring free. He was big and startlingly, deliciously wide. A little like his eyes right now, as they roved along her body. God, this was going to be good. This was Kyle. Big, bad, buff Kyle. The friend who had never, ever let her down.

The moment she spent anticipating was a moment too long, because Kyle took over again, and all her arms could do was snake up and out of the way. A strong, masculine hand flattened her on the bed then spent a long time on her torso.

"Nice," she purred.

"Nice?" he growled, letting his callused fingers rub her belly, then scoop along the curve of her breasts. A rumble built in his chest, and hell, if he wasn't shy about showing his pleasure, neither would she be.

"Great," she managed, giving in to the whimpering sounds building in her throat.

When his fingers explored her folds, then worked her from the inside, she surrendered completely. She climbed under his touch, writhing in pleasure.

His eyes swept upward to meet hers again, glowing yellowish blue like the outer edge of a bonfire—the parts that lapped around the edges of a charred log and threatened to consume it entirely.

"Stef," he murmured, and it was the groan of a bear who'd finally found his way to the honey.

She closed her eyes and gave herself over to the feel of him tasting her breasts, sampling her lips, exploring the walls of her sex. And through every singular sensation, she tried desperately to memorize it all. The tweak on her nipples, the pressure of his thumb over her clit. After the uncertainty of the past days, she thirsted for this solidity, this confidence.

Then it hit her. She'd been rolling with the punches of life instead of fighting back for too long. Maybe it was time to exercise a little control. Did she dare?

Dare, a voice urged. An animal voice deep inside her. One that felt like it belonged there.

Before she could lose her nerve, she sucked in a quick breath and led their bodies into a sideways roll until Kyle was prone beneath her, his eyes wide.

To hell with *forbidden.* She'd banish the thought from his mind. She kissed her way down his abdomen in a long, quick slide. Not that she wanted to miss any detail of his chiseled torso—but if she didn't go quickly, she might overthink what she was doing.

Enough thinking, her wolf nodded. *Trust the instincts that brought us to him.*

Her tongue was at his navel now, but she kept sliding down. She needed to take him in the light of day, to know it was her human side and not the beast doing the talking.

The thing was, she'd only ever taken a man in her mouth once in the past, and that hadn't been so much her own desire as the guy's request. Once had been enough, though, or so she'd always assumed.

Not any more. The burning need to do this—for herself, not just for him—possessed her.

Take our mate, the wolf inside her urged. *Show him what we can do.*

She eyed the crown of his cock then ducked closer until her lips greeted the glistening tip. His whole body hardened—a moment of truth. Would he let her take him like this?

Believe me, our mate wants this.

She shook inside but continued, whispering down the length of him, all the way into the curls of his groin and back up. God, he was long. Wide. Hard—for her. A tingle raced through her spine at the power she found in that moment. She licked the cleft of his velvety tip, first tentatively, then more insistently as her thoughts scattered to a thousand corners of her mind. North was full of heat; west was fiery as a sunset. South was churning with warm, wet anticipation, and east—east wanted her to hurry the hell along. This was her man, her home. She belonged here.

"Right there," he breathed, guiding her head.

Claim. Mate.

She opened wide and took him in one long, greedy gulp. Warm and solid as tensile steel, his cock filled her mouth and overpowered every sense but one.

Home.

Home tasted like the Southwest. Bold and tangy, big and fresh. Alive, as the rippling action of his abdomen told her. His fingers in her hair were screaming, *Yes, yes, yes.* She came up for a breath of air then swooped in again, determined to bring him to the very edge. One taste, then another, and another, until she was consuming him with desperate abandon.

"Stef," he whispered. Then all that came out of him was a throaty groan.

She fisted a hand around the base to keep up the rhythm when she pulled back and blew lightly. This was what she'd heard about but never experienced before. The sensual haze wasn't only his, but hers. The need to claim, to glory in her own power.

She'd never felt more alive, more capable. When her lips pulled back his foreskin and her tongue shot out to lap up the first dewy drops, the mountain under her moaned.

It really was him, trembling under her. It really was her, having the nerve to take it this far.

It really was love, powering it all.

Love, her wolf agreed. *Told you so.*

Chapter Twenty-Four

"Stef."

Kyle wasn't breathing, wasn't moving, except for his lips forming her name over and over. His fingers were threaded through her silky hair, trying hard not to clutch her closer or to push her away. Because Stef was taking him to a place way, way off the charts, where no woman had gone before. Where he never dared follow—until now.

"Right there," he breathed, thought, or groaned. Could have been any of the three.

He'd started with defenses a mile high that had PACK and DUTY graffitied all over them like a subway wall. The needy sheen in her eye set off an inner rumble, the first tremors of an earthquake. When her lips formed words—words like *yes* and *more*—the first fissures appeared. And when those lips touched down on him, the whole of the castle keep came tumbling down, one watchtower after another while he went deaf and blind to everything but the message coursing through his blood.

Mate. Mine.

He closed his eyes and gave himself over to the sliding sensation of her lips, the weight of her hands on his thighs. She took him deep then pulled up, tugging the foreskin before plunging back down and setting him flying on another rush. He heard the rattle of a shaky breath and knew it was his own. He was balanced on the razor's edge, wondering if any minute now the wolf would come ripping through his skin with a roar. The position was too submissive, too off guard for a wolf.

Like I'd go anywhere right now. The beast was lost in a lusty, helpless purr.

Stef came up for air and glanced his way, her lips glistening. "Is that good?"

"So good."

He managed that much before she formed a perfect O with her lips and closed over his cock, obliterating all thought. His world became a cascade of pleasure as she took him so far, he was teetering on the edge. That it was forbidden only added to the high. He was a kid on a carnival ride long after midnight, glorying in the rush.

You're supposed to be protecting her, not making things worse.

That's what he'd been told, but Christ, here he was, getting blown by her, getting ready to bury his balls deep in her welcoming body—center-of-the-earth deep. If that didn't provoke the North Ridge wolves, nothing would. But the entire desert seemed to be urging him into seventh heaven and for once, he wouldn't deny himself. She was his; he was hers. It was as simple as that—or at least simple enough for right now. He'd leave complicated for later—or better yet, never.

And yeah, he'd like to see Cody turn his back on a moment like this with his mate.

Just watch you don't fuck things up.

He wouldn't. He'd find a way to make it work. Somehow.

The thought gave him the willpower to jackknife up.

Stef sat back on her heels in surprise. "No good?"

"Too good." He pulled her in for a smothering kiss then broke off just long enough to explain. "But coming in your mouth is not where I want this to go."

The taste of him on her tongue set off his wolf again.

Take! Claim! Mine!

And not just the wolf, but his human side, too. *Mine!*

"And where do you want this to go?" she asked, her eyes sparkling with desire.

"Here," he grunted and rolled.

She came right with him, drawing her legs up along his thighs, locking her heels behind him. Whatever she did to shape those legs—running? biking? soccer?—worked because they were taut and sleek and roped with muscle. Aligning her body precisely with his and drawing him in.

"This okay?" he asked, pinning her arms over her head.

She smiled, sweet and sultry. "I haven't been this okay in a long time. Maybe never."

She arched her back, pushing the soft pillow of her breasts toward him. If anyone came along then to tell him *shouldn't* or *forbidden*, he'd throw them out a window. Because Stef was right in what she'd said. They were meant to be.

He slid in. A hundred exclamations knotted in his throat as she tightened around him. He nearly lost it right there but fought back the urge to release, focusing on the glow of her multicolored eyes. He wanted this to last an eternity, to get everything exactly right.

"Kyle," she groaned in a whole new note when he angled his hips, finding the perfect spot. His head bobbed over her nipples with every renewed thrust, bedding his cock deeper and deeper. He gave himself over completely to the interplay of hard and soft as her body first yielded, then clenched over every inch of his length. He wanted to fill her until there was no her and no him but only them. To purge the void inside himself and fill it with the comfort that was all her.

Harder, she begged. *Deeper.*

Was he was reading it on her lips or hearing it in his mind?

Take me, he could swear he heard as Stef angled her head to one side.

The sight of the smooth white flesh of her exposed neck made his canines pinch against his gums. He ran a hungry tongue over the emerging points of his fangs.

One bite! One bite was all it would take to claim her as his own. All of this would be finished. All the loneliness, the emptiness in his life.

Mate! his wolf screamed as he dipped closer.

Thu-thump. Thu-thump. He could feel the blood rushing under her skin. His teeth extended and scraped over her neck, honing in on their mark.

Yes! his wolf crowed, and a thousand spirit wolves with it. *Claim!*

He was dipping his head the last hair's breadth when a single defiant voice cried out.

Stop!

If his thoughts had been playing out in a theater, a thousand heads would have whirled around. It was the squeaky voice of a boy facing a foe greater than himself. The boy he'd once been.

No! the boy cried. *Not if you only want this for yourself!*

His inner wolf snickered. *She wants it, too! Look at her beg!*

You're no better than him! the boy shouted.

An icy cold gripped his mind. Did the boy mean his stepfather? Did he mean Ron, the man who attacked Stefanie?

I'll show you better than Ron, his wolf grumbled, retracting his fangs.

Yes, the boy whispered. *Show me. Do it right.*

"Kyle," Stef breathed. "Don't stop."

He swept aside the boy and the wolf and focused on the sweet friction along his cock as it slid against the ridges of her inner walls. Focused on Stefanie, who called his name over and over. On the pinch in his balls telling him he was close, blissfully close. When she convulsed around him, her climax shaking her hard, his wolf roared and he thrust madly, losing his rhythm. His vision flashed and his hips jerked. One push, two, and he shattered inside her, coming with his own throaty groan.

He heard her murmuring, telling him how good it felt, her voice modulating as a second wave of pleasure shook her, then a third. He stroked her hair, losing himself in her glow of her skin. He'd emptied himself into her, but all he felt was full—full of something sweet and rare.

When Stef opened her eyes, the colors swirled in delight. The honest brown, the earthy green, the hopeful gray, all of it blending and separating like a kaleidoscope. She smiled a shy smile then leaned forward to meet his lips.

He gloried in the honesty of that kiss. It wasn't the triumphant glory of a bite, but it felt right—righter than the bite would have been, at least tonight. He settled for a thousand kisses and the promise of later, gazing down the length of her body as her breath came hard and fast. The points of her nipples were rising and falling like a tide. She was so beautiful, so perfect.

So... his.

"Hey, you," she whispered, running a finger over his lips.

He kissed it. "Hey, you."

Slowly, carefully, he settled down over her. Her body curling into his set off a low, steady buzz, and the way she wrapped her arms around his neck told him she never wanted to let go.

Just as slowly and carefully, Kyle closed his eyes and looked to his inner wolf. Would the beast be greedy for more? Triumphant? Possessive? He peered beyond the pleasure flooding him and past that inner door.

And damned if the beast wasn't curled in a ball, thumping his tail in sheer contentment. The greed was replaced by something a whole lot... softer. Kinder. Mushier, if that was the word.

What are you thinking? he asked the wolf, suddenly suspicious.

The wolf gave a deep sigh, and the image of a couple of brown-eyed, brown-haired pups popped into Kyle's mind. Cute and fluffy and helpless without his love.

Pups. Good idea. The wolf nodded then broke into a lazy yawn.

Kyle reeled in surprise, stuck between a chuckle and a heady sigh. He risked a peek into the muted light of his bedroom, worried that daylight would bring all this to a crashing end. Some ugly truth would be revealed, Stefanie would bury her head in shame and regret, and this impossible vision would slip away once more.

But the sun was still shining, the room bright and hopeful. Stef was draped over him like she'd had a decade to find her favorite spot and not just a couple of days. He reached out with a finger, waiting for the mirage to pop and dissipate, but it didn't. Her muscles were hard, her flesh real, the truth hale and hearty. He wondered when he'd last felt this good, when the house had ever felt so full of... something. Something nice.

"Maybe," Stefanie whispered, fingers strumming the line of his ribs.

He combed his fingers through her hair, twirling it into a bun. "Maybe?"

"Probably," she mused.

Probably what? He cupped one side of her face in his hand, looking into her eyes.

She smiled back, nodding. "Definitely."

"Definitely?"

Her smile stretched. "Definitely all grown up."

He gave a tiny nod so she'd go on.

"As a kid, I never wanted to let that happen. But now, I kind of like it." She smiled, a little mischievous, rubbing her chin against his chest.

He chuckled. "Yeah, I kind of like it too."

"Yeah?" She studied him closely.

"Yeah." He pulled her close.

Though *kind of* didn't come close to the truth. They were meant for each other, and he was all in. No matter what kind of trouble came their way.

The curtain flapped in agreement with both sentiments: that this was the real thing, and that trouble was sure to be lurking somewhere not too far away.

Chapter Twenty-Five

Stefanie was still floating on a silken cloud when a movement registered in her mind. She mumbled, finding Kyle's skin with her lips, and sighed herself back to sleep. But there it was again, the shift of his muscles beside her.

She cracked an eye open. The room was warm as summer, cozy as winter, and it could have been either given the way the slanting sun was making the curtains glow. Late afternoon, she thought lazily and felt a smile spread at the realization. Because now she knew. Being with Kyle was a function of her human heart, not just a trick of the night. She'd spent a happy hour snoozing on that idea, and even the color of sunset couldn't change her mind.

"Stef," Kyle whispered. The sound of his voice like his body: all the softness in it had gone rock hard. "Stay here," he grunted, rolling away.

She reached for him, too late. He couldn't be leaving her now, could he?

She wanted to call out his name, but the sound caught in her throat. Kyle was listening at the door, naked, every muscle defined as his nostrils tested the air. He glanced back, and the look on his face scared the hell out of her.

That look said *I will die for you,* and he meant now.

She scrambled up beside him to peer out. Lights filled the driveway along with the sound of tires crunching over gravel, the squeak of misaligned brakes. They had company.

"Stay there," he said, his voice an octave lower than usual. He pushed her gently back, slipped out, and pulled the door closed.

141

She stared at the doorknob in shock. What was going on? She grabbed the shirt laying on the floor and yanked it over her head then followed him outside. As soon as she stepped out onto the porch, she froze in her tracks. Even with the sunset glinting off the windshield of the truck outside, she knew exactly who was inside.

Ron. Greer. They'd come for her.

Kyle hustled her off the porch and over to the side of his truck then fumbled with the driver's side door. He cursed when it jammed, and they both whirled at the sudden silence behind them.

Ron slid out of the truck and approached with the easy step of a welcome visitor. For all of two steps, that is, until Kyle growled in a warning.

Stef wished she could be a cobra; now would be her time to strike. She'd spit her poison at Ron and get this nightmare over with for good.

"Leave," she barked, packing the word with all the venom she could muster.

"Please, Stefanie." Ron spread his arms wide, the very picture of an unjustly wronged man. "I'm here to take you home."

Right. Home.

Behind him, the mountain that was Greer unfolded his body from the truck, making a show of stretching to his full height in a slow, bristling process. If she hadn't known the word *alpha*, she was sure it would have popped into her mind.

"We got tired of waiting for the elders to decide," Greer said.

"Got nervous, you mean," Kyle shot back.

Testosterone filled the air and a standoff ensued. She tried not to shiver. Kyle formed a solid wall in front of her while Ron stood with the confidence of a sheep who knew the farmer was guarding his back with a shotgun aimed squarely at the wolf. Greer, meanwhile, threw Kyle a look of dismissal. Clearly, he expected Kyle to back down.

Only Kyle didn't budge. He snarled. "Back off. Now."

Ron reached a hand out, palm up. "Stefanie. Come home with me."

She snorted out loud. Home was right here.

"You belong with me," Ron said over Kyle's continuous growl.

Like hell I do. She wanted to shout but couldn't quite form the words. Out of the blue, her side was cramping. It was only Kyle's hand on her arm that kept her from doubling over.

Ron flipped his fingers in a *come here* motion, and a thousand tiny needles jabbed her ribs.

"Yes," Ron hissed. "Come."

Kyle threw an arm in front of her, blocking her path. "Never!"

Stef was shocked to find herself leaning forward, as if she wanted to step forward and take his hand. Her insides were churning; everything was propelling her forward.

The need will start to pull you in.

God, was it true? Her eyes stung, her heart fluttered and she felt—Christ, did she really want him? Ron?

A wave of nausea rolled over her. She was getting pulled in by some invisible force, and the only thing stopping it was the thick muscle of Kyle's arm against her chest.

"Get in the car," he grunted, every inch of him poised for a fight.

That was enough to break the invisible grip Ron seemed to have over her—that, and the shove Kyle gave her toward the front of the car. She wrenched the handle to the passenger's side open and scrambled inside. She slid across the seat, found the keys, and started the engine with a roar. When she slammed on the gas pedal, the wheels spun madly and sent gravel flying like shrapnel. She could feel the pull of Ron even as she sped off. She'd nearly walked to her own doom. If it hadn't been for Kyle, she would have—

Her thoughts collided with a brick wall. Kyle. She'd felt a pull toward him, too. She hunched over the steering wheel, her stomach heaving. God, what did it mean? She thought that their lovemaking was the result of an attraction that was pure and good. But what if it wasn't? Maybe Ron's bite had set off something in her body that had her lusting after the closest source of testosterone. Kyle. Ron. Greer. What if she wasn't able to distinguish them any more?

She flew around the next bend so fast, both right wheels lifted off the ground. The truck nearly skidded out when the tires hit the ground again. She fought the vehicle back under control then rolled the window down to gulp fresh air. The enemy wasn't just the men back there. The enemy was within.

Escape. Was there any escape from the beast she had become?

Chapter Twenty-Six

Kyle listened to the truck thunder away in an explosion of sound and motion, feeling like a man who'd been trampled by a herd of bison. Or maybe that was just his heart being dragged under the spinning wheels of the Chevy. He could feel every chunk of gravel, every sharp-edged rock along the way.

His soul wailed to see her go, but his wolf just saw the red of anger.

Kill these bastards. Now.

Sending Stef away went against every instinct, but what else could he do? His chances of beating Greer outright were slim. The best he could do was buy Stefanie time to escape.

The grim hope must have been stamped on his face because Greer sneered. "We found her once. We'll find her again."

"You. Will. Not. Have. Her."

He clenched his jaw so hard, it clicked. But Greer was right. Stef's blood would call to Ron and they'd find her, wherever she was. She'd never be safe, unless she were claimed by another wolf with a second bite that would supersede Ron's imprint and free her from his hold.

Kyle waited for his inner wolf to shout that he could have been the one. That he should have claimed her when he had the chance. But the wolf seemed quiet on that matter; even he seemed to accept that it wouldn't have been right. Not until she was ready.

But now, he'd never get the chance. He felt it in every choked breath that signaled the growing distance between him and his destined mate. Stefanie was the one.

And she was racing away.

Let them try to find her. Let them try to get past me. His wolf bristled, scratching to get out.

He forced a breath past the lump in his throat and faced Greer. "What kind of pack do you run that you have to recruit by force?"

The man just scoffed. "Women don't know what's best for them."

He could have let a fist fly right there. "You are sick."

His wolf grinned inside. *So let's play doctor and fix him up. Starting with ripping his lungs out.*

The North Ridge alpha was eyeing him, nostrils flaring, making the most of his intimidating bulk. Greer had a good three inches over him and a significant weight advantage—not to mention a backup man.

Kyle's eyelid twitched. If only he'd acted on the impulse to bite her. Even if he died in this fight, Stef would have been free of Ron's hold.

He ground his teeth. It was time to think, not regret. Anything to save his mate.

Speed was his only chance. His canines pinched the back of his gums, and this time, he didn't bother holding them back. He growled, ready to make his stand.

Greer raised a finger toward Kyle's bare chest. "Nice print," he taunted, pointing at the scars. "Let me guess. You're the cop who got nicked by our biker boy."

His skin burned at the mention of the fight that had turned his life upside down. Nicked? He'd nearly bled dry. But how would Greer know about the fight that had turned him? Unless. . .

The alpha was nodding, looking ridiculously pleased. "Yeah, he was one of ours. A rogue. I tried to stop him, I really did," he said, dripping insincerity.

If Greer had wanted to stop a wolf from leaving North Ridge and going rogue, he would have. Clearly, he hadn't bothered.

"What kind of alpha lets one of his own go rogue?" Kyle asked, infusing his voice with an evenness he didn't feel. A good alpha would hunt the rogue down before his home pack could be discredited. Before the rogue could claim any innocent victims.

Kyle had taken weeks to heal. Afterward, he'd hunted far and wide for the perpetrator but come up empty. The rogue could be anywhere, hurting anyone. Who knew how many victims had he claimed? Innocent lives? Not to mention putting all shifters at risk if his true nature were exposed.

Greer laughed. "What do you know about being an alpha?"

Kyle flashed his teeth. "I know an alpha looks out for more than himself."

"Says the man who beds another's mate," Greer shot back.

Of course, the man could smell Stefanie's scent on him. Well, let him. Ron, too.

"My mate," he growled.

"Twin Moon pack will pay for your transgression," Greer said, letting his voice drop to a threat.

"She was attacked!" Kyle barked.

"She's mine!" Ron insisted.

Kyle unleashed a roar that came from a place deeper than his lungs. "She's mine!" The words echoed through the hollow, and the silence that followed was deathly still.

Ron trembled, but Greer had never looked happier. "So you challenge Ron?"

"I challenge you," he retorted.

Greer grinned in smug delight, and Kyle realized he'd been maneuvered into handing the alpha a golden opportunity. It wasn't Greer challenging him; it was him, challenging Greer. Superficially, it would appear that he was at fault: taking a woman who belonged to North Ridge, then fighting the alpha over her for no reason but his own greed. Greer would kill him, hunt Stefanie down, then frame Kyle as the bad guy. And after that, who knew? Greer might even demand more from Twin Moon pack for the damage he'd claim Kyle inflicted on his female "property."

Kyle shook his head, watching the gears tick over behind Greer's eyes. The man was smarter than he looked. And he, Kyle, was a fool for letting his destined mate and his pack down.

Greer smiled like he held all the trumps in the last hand of a poker game. He stepped into motion, making a show of examining Kyle.

"Mmm, she smells good, even on you." He followed up with an expression of mock surprise. "But wait! If you screwed her, she could be pregnant. Just think."

Kyle's heart skipped a beat. He hadn't had time to think anything of the sort. Things between him and Stefanie had moved so fast, and there were so many other complications. . .

Greer's face twisted into a cruel smile. "Such a pity to have to kill an unborn thing, don't you think? But don't worry, if there is one, I'll make sure to replace it with my own."

A shock wave ripped through his body. He knew Greer was only trying to rile him, but. . . What if? Anger like he'd never known flooded him. His wolf claws emerged from their sheaths and dug into his palms.

You will never have my mate.

More than anything, he wanted to jump Greer now. To rip him apart and scatter the pieces far and wide. But he had to fight smart. He was taking on a powerful alpha who would show no mercy, take no prisoners.

And right now, playing smart meant buying time for Stef. He needed to stay cool if he was to somehow win this fight.

Watch me, his wolf snarled.

Greer's smug face contorted and stretched as the wolf emerged from the man. In the same moment, Kyle went from statue to living hell, snarling into his own shift.

On the sideline, Ron stood sneering, and his unspoken words shot into the night.

Let the fight begin.

Chapter Twenty-Seven

Stefanie pulled the truck out of a wild skid then floored the gas pedal again. Far and fast was all she could focus on. But where could she go? Even if she eluded Ron and Greer, she'd never escape herself, no matter how many miles she covered in Kyle's truck.

If she could crawl out of her own skin, she would. Ron had barely flicked his fingers at her, and she'd been drawn to him like a marionette. Worse still was the possibility that the same force had drawn her to Kyle's bed. Were some crazy wolf hormones telling her to mate—with anyone? She kept one hand on the steering wheel; the other scratched fiercely at her leg.

Every mile tore another thread from her heart. That warm, safe sensation she'd had with Kyle—was it all an illusion? If Ron bit her again and claimed her, would she believe she liked it? She would become one of those kidnapping victims who was brainwashed by her captors. Brainwashed, or maybe bloodwashed: whatever word shifters might use to describe the ghastly phenomenon.

Lights flashed ahead, and she jammed on the brakes, screeching right up to the edge of the highway. The sky was bloodied and bruised, the clouds pierced by slanting bolts of sunset. She let the pickup idle briefly before collecting her nerves and swinging into a squealing left turn, heading south. The humming sound of tires over smooth asphalt gradually slowed her racing pulse. She forced in a long yoga breath and glanced at the sky, picking out the first stars of the night. The W of Cassiopeia was emerging from the indigo of space and she cocked her head, remembering how right it had looked. The stars had given her hope. They'd led her to Kyle.

Mate.

Her throat thickened just thinking about him. Right now, the W of the constellation looked sad and droopy. Distinctly... not right, and worse with every mile she traveled. It shouldn't be possible to notice a change like that within a short drive, but she was sure of it.

But south had to be the best way to head—right? The question flickered in the arc of the headlights, along with so many others. Where to go? Who to trust?

Kyle. We can trust him, the wolf said inside. *Mate.*

She didn't know what was right. Only that leaving Kyle was wrong.

Another deep breath brought her a trace of his scent, and her body immediately warmed. She tried ignoring the sensation, but then allowed herself another tentative sniff. Analyzing, wondering, considering the possibilities.

Kyle's scent is nothing like Ron's, the wolf huffed. *And neither is our attraction to him.*

It was true. Kyle was like the sun: pure, warm, clean. With Ron, there'd been the suck of quicksand, a feeling of encroaching darkness. Ron set off nothing but pain, as if all the cells in her body had gotten on their hands and knees to claw their way away from him.

Because he's a monster. I know my mate, the wolf insisted. *You know him, too. You've known him for a long time.*

She straightened in her seat, dissecting every interaction with Kyle over the past few days, then looking further back in time. It was true; the pull had always been there, long before this nightmare started. Kyle had been a friend until fate reunited them and appointed him her guide into the foreign world of shapeshifters. Her protector. Her lover. How could her attraction to him be wrong?

She pulled over to the shoulder of the highway and tilted her head back, looking at the stars. The patterns seemed skewed, as if she'd gone too far. As if the right place was where she'd just come from. Twin Moon Ranch—the very western edge of it, to be exact. Where Kyle was right now.

Home.

The truth came to her in a flood. Kyle: her love for him was all human, all her. She wasn't turning into a wild beast. She'd just found the right man at the wrong time.

Then why turn your back on your mate? came the angry voice of her wolf.

For the first time, she thought of it that way: her wolf. She and the wolf were one, just as she and Kyle were one.

Her eyes flicked to the rearview mirror as her hands tightened on the wheel. In one quick maneuver, she peeled the truck into a scream of a U-turn and hit the gas, heading back to the fight.

Chapter Twenty-Eight

She drove in a strange state of elation. No matter that Ron and Greer were there. It was Kyle who mattered. Kyle and the pack.

It was her fault they were in danger. She'd brought the menace of North Ridge pack here; she had to stay and finish what she was responsible for starting.

Or die trying, her wolf added.

That gave her the strength to do it—her wolf. That and the shame of leaving Kyle while she turned tail and ran. She leaned over the steering wheel, coaxing the truck along like a team of horses. An upward glance confirmed that yes, the stars were smiling now, telling her this was right. At the turn, she pulled off the highway and hammered over dirt as fast as she dared. Flying off the crest of each rise, she pushed the vehicle to its limits until finally, Kyle's house was in front of her. The hair on her arms stood erect when she made a wide arc around Greer's car and let the headlights capture the scene.

Two wolves stood facing each other like a couple of vicious razorbacks, both throwing bristling shadows that doubled their size. Neither so much as flicked an ear at the truck, so engrossed were they in the fight. Teeth bared and glistening, they circled each other slowly, looking for an opening.

She recognized Kyle immediately, even as a wolf. It wasn't just the spiky hair or the tint of his coat; it was the power and economy of movement that struck her. The wary countenance of his body was the same—the same, she realized, going all the way back to when she'd first met him at fourteen. He'd been just a kid then, a kid who'd had a hard start. But he'd grown up to make something of himself, all on his own.

Her heart leaped. Kyle the wolf was just like Kyle the man, hiding pain and loneliness behind a mask of detachment. And when his eyes turned to her, she knew. She was sure.

Mate. Mine.

Her next breath—and the one after that, and the one after that—was deeper, richer. Cleaner.

Greer was the other wolf. Huge and haughty. The favorite son of some bully of an alpha, she guessed, who'd never considered anyone but himself. She let her lips curl in a snarl. He was a dark gray color that should have been striking but for the dullness of it, so unlike the sheen of Kyle's coat. Kyle's wolf drew her eye just as the man did. But she ached to see darker patches along his body, where he was bloody and torn. She could make out a clumpy line along his flank and another along his shoulder. Not that Greer had gone unscathed: his coat was mottled with dark patches too, if not as many as Kyle's.

Let Kyle concentrate on Greer. We have to take out Ron.

But where was he? She tore her eyes from Kyle and scanned the yard. She could never fight Greer—even Kyle's odds were slim against that hulk—but maybe, just maybe, she could fight Ron. Or hold him off, at least, until...until... She shook her head; the plan didn't extend beyond there.

Her eyes automatically searched for a hunchback of a wolf, but the figure she found cowering behind Greer was Ron in human form. He was holding something in his hands, keeping just out of reach.

Coward.

Her confidence rose a notch. She didn't know anything about fighting or wolves, but she had a couple of weapons of her own. Anger was one, because she was simmering with it. Ron was the one who started this, and Ron would pay. She had courage, too, a currency Ron would never have. The courage to stand by her mate and fight for what was right. To fight for a future.

For our future, her wolf agreed.

If anger and courage didn't see her through this night, nothing would.

The minute she slid out of the truck, the bassline of the wolves' continuous snarls rumbled through her body. She set her shoulders wide and circled around the wolves, making for Ron.

Coming back for your mate? A deep voice jeered; that could only be Greer.

Yes, she thought, eyes pinned on Kyle. *Mate.*

She didn't dare distract him, though. Instead, she focused on Ron. That was her fight.

The man had the audacity to smile. *Stefanie. You've come back to me.*

The words popped into her mind, clear as a bell, and she could feel the inner scrape again, the sound of nails scratching against a chalkboard as her body responded to his pull. But this time, she was ready for it. Though her eyes were on Ron, her mind held tight to an image of Kyle. This time, she could resist.

Not that she let on to Ron. He'd played dirty back in Colorado, attacking her out of the blue. She wasn't above doing the same.

Let that bastard get a taste of his own medicine.

She took another step, trying to project weakness while clinging to the courage inside. Ron held his hand out, waving her closer, and despite what it cost her pride, she approached. One step. Two. She could see a smile play across his lips as his canines emerged.

Greer and Kyle erupted into a whirl of ferocious noise punctuated by vicious snarls, making her scuttle aside. Her ribs registered a sharp twinge, and her first thought was that Ron was drawing her in again. Then she realized this was different: the pain was real. Her eyes flipped to Kyle. Was he hurt?

It took everything she had not to cry out his name. Kyle was hurt, but she had to focus on Ron. He held a rope in his hands, and his fingers played over the braided strands. He'd been planning to trip Kyle up, it seemed, or otherwise interfere with the fight.

She saw something else, too. Not a yard from Ron's right side, an ax protruded from a stump. If she could get to it. . .

There was another outburst from the wolves, and when Ron glanced their way, she rushed forward and yanked the ax free. The weight of it felt strange in her hands now that it was a weapon and not a tool, and the most she could manage was a wild swing.

Ron skittered out of the way and pulled his focus back to her, eyes narrowing.

Bitch.

She heard that clearly, too, and stepped closer, undeterred.

"Try vengeful bitch, asshole."

Ron's dark eyes went wide. "Stefanie," he barked, trying on the voice of command. "Stop this nonsense and come with me."

She widened her grip and raised the ax, gauging its heft, then took an experimental swing. *Whoosh!* It sliced through the air, and Ron's eyes went wide. She let out a grunt. *There, that's better.*

"I will never come with you."

She was about to take another swing when Greer and Kyle sprang into motion. They rolled in a heap, booming in anger and pain. They wrestled and snapped, and Greer brought all his weight to bear on Kyle. She felt the twinge again and knew it was him, howling inside from a couple of broken ribs. He was fighting back, but his strength was ebbing under the onslaught.

The next thing she knew, she was charging Kyle's way, brandishing the ax at Greer. She felt nothing, thought nothing, concentrating entirely on her enemy.

"Greer!" Ron shouted in warning.

Greer twisted off Kyle just in time to leap clear of her blade. Kyle scrambled for his footing; Stef saw that much before she stumbled and found herself facing Greer head-on. His wolf jaws were red and bloody, his eyes wild, and she froze, helpless as a mouse before a python. Then thunder roared in her ears and everything became a blur. She was falling, rolling, struggling to her feet. Kyle had shoved ahead of her, blocking Greer, ready to take up the fight. Another bout of wolf snarling began, its epicenter not two yards away, the timbre decidedly lower, more dangerous than before.

Breathe! She struggled to control her feet. *Think!*

But she lost her footing and everything went wrong from there. At her yelp, Kyle whipped around to check on her just as something came hurtling from out of the shadows. Ron had tossed a log to Greer, who shifted into human form behind Kyle. His paw stretched into a hand just in time to catch the log and bring it crashing down on Kyle's head. Stef choked out a garbled warning, but it was too late. A blur of brown, a dull thump, and Kyle crumpled.

"No!" she screamed as Greer clubbed Kyle a second time. He was preparing for a third strike before she could act, lurching forward to stop him. But Ron body checked her aside, and Greer struck again.

With strength she didn't know she had, she shoved Ron away and jumped toward her fallen mate. "Kyle!" He lay terrifyingly still, blood running down his muzzle, eyes closed.

Greer—in human form now—rose like a giant over Kyle's prone wolf, grinning in triumph. His eyes raked over her, his naked body showing his greed.

"Stefanie," he said, all cat to the mouse. "Such a pleasure to see a woman with spunk." The spark in his eyes told her exactly what kind of pleasure he had in mind.

She bit back a disgusted cry. The man was a brute, a barbarian. This was an alpha? A leader? He was nothing like Ty, the Twin Moon alpha, who tempered his raw power with a steady, fair hand, nor anything like Cody, with his diplomat's voice and kind eyes. Those men knew what duty and honor meant. This man was a monster.

Shift, her wolf demanded. *Let me out.*

She batted the thought away. She could barely coordinate four feet; she'd be useless as a wolf. Somehow, she'd have to think her way out of this. But how?

Giving herself up to the North Ridge wolves was a repulsive proposition and would do nothing for Kyle. They'd kill him as he lay unconscious even if she surrendered. She eyed the distance to the house and the phone inside. She could call for help. The pack would help her... wouldn't they?

Greer seemed to read her mind. "I'll huff and I'll puff," he chuckled.

She wished she could come up with a cutting remark to put the man in his place. "You're no man," she snarled. "No wolf." Because she got it now. There were wolves of honor just like there were men of honor. But there were cowards, lowlifes, and opportunists, too.

She expected him to attack, but Greer only kicked some dust at Ron's feet. "Get moving, idiot. Get your mate...if you can."

That mocking tone was also unlike anything she had heard at Twin Moon Ranch. Obviously fate had led her to the right place.

Her wolf nodded inside. *Destiny.*

Ron looked suddenly nervous, Greer strangely excited. The alpha crossed his arms over his chest and thrust out his chin. "I think I might even enjoy watching this."

With that, he turned to the stump and sat, ready to be entertained.

Chapter Twenty-Nine

Stef knew she should hold her tongue, but she couldn't. "You are sick," she said to Greer, even as she brought the ax up to ward off an advancing Ron.

She swung, but the weight of the ax head got away from her, and Ron easily sidestepped the blow.

Breathe, she tried. *Ready. . .*

She braced her legs to take another swing—on target this time—but stopped at the sudden cramp in her side. Ron's eyes narrowed in glee, and her stomach knotted. It was happening again—his pull was sucking her closer.

Greer laughed, enjoying the show. At least his mind was off Kyle. Stef glanced at the prone form, wondering if there had been a flicker of movement in his ear. She tightened her grip on the ax as Ron came straight at her, fists raised.

His tobacco scent assaulted her first, and she swung wildly. Ron ducked and grabbed for the ax, but she managed to twist it away. It happened once, twice, but each time she was a little too late, a little too hesitant. Her arms were tiring fast, and Ron's fangs were starting to show, reminding her of the horrible day that started all this.

She fought on, and Greer clapped when she got in a siding blow that knocked Ron to the ground.

"Bitch," Ron growled, heaving to his feet. "You will come with me." The red in his eyes dared her to try again.

Enough with the sissy hits.

She twisted the ax handle in her hands so that the blade faced her enemy as she barreled at him. Ron was faster than she expected, though; he caught the handle and grappled for control. Greer was cheering, Ron snarling, her body screaming

159

inside. Her strength was no match for Ron's, and he forced the ax away. Hands were yanking her hair, clawing her skin, and suddenly, he had her pinned to the ground, his fangs coming at her. Every muscle in her body kicked and flailed in desperate defense.

No! No! No! her wolf and human sides screamed as one.

There was a little bump at the edge of her mind, a stirring. Kyle! It had to be him, struggling back to consciousness. But she couldn't wait for his help; right now, she was the only one who could save them both.

Yet nothing she did could hold Ron back. A greedy murmur sounded beside her ear as he closed in.

The first bite turns, the second bite mates.

The drool of hot saliva seared her throat as Ron's teeth scraped along her skin, honing in on their mark.

Then a cloud drifted free of the moon, and the pale light washed over the landscape. Something tore through her. A roar filled the night, and just like that, she was a spectator, watching a brown-haired, brown-eyed wolf rip its way from under Ron's grip. The wolf instantly launched into a counter-attack, knowing just where to bite and when to twist, how to coordinate four feet and a pair of jaws that felt mighty and powerful.

Stefanie lived it all, because she was the wolf, taking her fury out on her attacker.

Don't just watch, the wolf cried. *Help me!*

That's all it took; she was all in. Not just a witness, but a fighter in her own right.

Ron's eyes went wide as she jumped at his exposed neck. Then all she saw was his fur, close up. She tasted blood gushing between her jaws and held on even as bile rose in her throat. It was two against one: she and her wolf against the man who started her nightmare. She braced her legs and held on and on until he ceased struggling and the last dribble of blood slowed. Then, with a grating click, her jaws released her foe.

She stood over the body, swaying. There would be no victory shake, no celebration. She spit, disgusted with Ron and with herself. Even in death, he'd forced her to do what she didn't want to do: to kill. Still, she was no beast. Not like him.

Her wolf managed a weary grin. *There are wolves, and there are wolves, you know.*

She knew. She finally knew.

When she looked up, Greer was watching her closely, still in his human form. Still naked. Clearly, the fight had been to his taste, because every muscle on him stood out from the flesh, aroused.

"Well done, she-wolf." He applauded. "You've proven yourself worthy of a better mate."

She could have howled in despair. She'd just killed a man, and for what? The next barbarian was already in line—and this one, she could never best.

There was a movement behind Greer. The wind, maybe, rippling through the bush?

"I like this new arrangement," Greer went on. "Why borrow you from a fool when I can have you for myself?"

A wave of nausea swept over her, and she shot a protest right into his mind. *You will never have me!*

She forced her stiff legs to back away, but Greer was already upon her, his hands rough, his voice greedy. All she could do was close her eyes and hope for death because living a life imposed on her by Greer was too horrible to consider.

But she couldn't just wish herself to death, and Greer clearly wanted her alive. With one hand in her hair and the other locking her wrists, he yanked her head back to expose her neck.

The end, she thought.

But just as his fangs touched down on her skin, there was a bone-jarring jolt and a howl, and she was thrown flat on her back. The air churned over her, filled with screams and wild flailing. Time rushed forward then shuddered to a stop when she realized there were no more clamping hands, no teeth, no bad breath—only a glimpse of sky full of the purest, cleanest blue. Blue that felt like home.

That blue was far too angry to be the sky, and the sun had long since set.

That blue was Kyle's eyes boring into hers, begging for recognition. His feet bracketed her body, keeping her safe.

Mine, her wolf cried. *Mate.*

The gold in Kyle's eyes flared like a sunspot, and she heard his response.

Mine. Mate.

She would have given anything to relish the moment, but he was already twisting away. How he fought past his injuries, she didn't know, only that he had found a second wind. His wolf was a whirlwind of sheer determination that went at Greer with a fury even the mighty alpha couldn't match. She struggled back to her feet and leaped into the fray.

Greer had shifted back into wolf form but couldn't quite land his blows, while Kyle was everywhere, slashing and tearing until he'd worked his way into Greer's thick ruff. Stef worked the outside, snapping at Greer's flank and legs. It didn't do much, but it was enough for Kyle to find a hold.

Greer gave a strange yelp, and she saw death register on his face, first in a flash of disbelief, then denial. His hind legs scratched at the ground until a glaze came over his eyes and he went limp. Kyle held on a long time then gave the body a mighty shake before dropping it unceremoniously to the ground. He stood panting over the vanquished alpha then slowly raised his eyes to hers. Her breath caught, and for all the bloody images sickening her soul, there was warmth, too.

They took one slow step toward each other, and she rushed through the rest when he crumpled to the ground, utterly spent.

Kyle! It came out as an anguished yelp.

She circled him, letting her fur brush his. Just as she'd let her wolf take over in the fight, she let it care for Kyle now, licking his bloodstained neck in long, careful strokes. She sniffed him, begging for some sign.

Please be okay. Please be okay...

Panic built when he didn't reply, until a voice registered in her mind, weary and distant. *I'm okay. But if I tell you, you might stop, and this feels too good.*

Jesus. Had she been in human form, she might have sung her joy, but her wolf settled for a thin whine and licked on. Kyle tasted of blood and grit and desert sand, but under it all, she tasted pure relief.

Mate. My mate.

She curled around him and closed her eyes, blocking away the heavy shadows of the night while she counted the beats of his heart. For a time, that was her whole world, that cocoon of him and her and the night. Her and her mate.

But soon, too soon, the desert stirred. Her head popped up. There was movement out there, an approaching mass. One moment, it was just her and Kyle, and the next, a riot of frenzied voices was breaking on to the scene. The Twin Moon wolves had arrived.

About fucking time, she thought she heard Kyle think. But there was a soft edge to the complaint; even she knew how far the ranch was. How they even knew to come was a mystery to her. But if Kyle could push his thoughts into her mind, he could probably send them over distances, too.

She curled herself tighter around Kyle and did her best not to growl too openly at anyone who came close. It was his pack; they'd do him no harm. But the fighting instinct was still in her veins, and she wasn't ready to trust anyone. And she certainly wasn't part of the pack. She stiffened, wondering what would happen next.

A dark, brooding presence that could only be Ty swept past, sniffing Kyle, then moving on to Greer. Stef let her head pop up to study him, suddenly fearful. She and Kyle had just killed two members of another pack. What consequences would there be?

The din faded to a hush as the others took stock of the scene, anxious and subdued. One wolf let out a mournful whine while another licked Kyle's fur. As one wolf after another came by, snuffling anxiously, she could sense relief and elation fill the air. Kyle's packmates had been worried for him. Deeply worried. But he was all right, and she could practically hear the collective exhale.

163

She rubbed him with her muzzle, reinforcing the message. He had a home—a real home with an honest pack whose members held him dear. Did he get it?

Kyle's head bobbed, and she imagined him gulping hard away his emotions. Maybe he was more a part of this pack than he'd ever dared to imagine. Maybe he finally saw himself as something more than an outsider. Because the message coming from all the wolves around them said the same thing: he belonged.

His eyes closed, but she could sense his heart swell. Yeah, he got it, all right.

She glanced around as more wolves and a handful of humans approached. Some of the faces were familiar, others new. There was an Amazon of a woman with a bow in her hand, and the arrow notched in the string had a silver tip. She frowned and approached Greer's body slowly. Only after a kick did the woman slowly let down her guard.

"He's dead, Rae," someone assured her.

"Better be." Rae's voice was gruff.

Stef wondered who Rae was, and what Greer had done to earn her spite. If the man was so obviously hated, though, maybe she wouldn't be in such big trouble for playing a role in his death. Did she dare hope?

A pair of human feet appeared at her side, and Cody's happy-go-lucky voice immediately put her at ease. "Playing possum, Kyle?"

Stefanie heard Kyle's weak rumble. *Can't a guy nurse his wounds?*

"I'd say your she-wolf is doing that."

Stefanie felt Kyle tighten into a laugh then choke at the pain in his ribs. She slid her body right, nudging Cody out of the way. What Kyle needed now was time to heal. Peace.

Peace, and you. His unspoken words filled her with warmth.

Cody chuckled and moved away. "All right, all right, I get the picture. He needs a little more nursing, right?"

A lot more, she couldn't help but add as Cody winked at the champagne-colored female brushing along his side, whisking her tail in approval.

Kyle let out a low rumble of agreement and relaxed into her frame. She felt the weight of him, pressing into her side, and decided she'd never felt quite that good.

Don't worry, she pushed the thought his way. *I'll keep you.*

Keep me? Kyle murmured in mock protest.

Keep you safe, she replied, snuggling her body alongside his.

Epilogue

Ten months later...

Kyle bent over the stack of mesquite and loaded up his arms then made for the bonfire pit. He had to weave around half a dozen packmates to do so, all of them scurrying with preparations for the summer solstice: a day the pack celebrated with a barbecue of epic proportions. There'd be games for young and old alike, followed by a feast. The meat of six Angus steer had been slow-roasting in an earth oven overnight, packed in canvas sacks soaked with hickory-scented barbecue sauce. The steak would come out tender and juicy; a real treat. That would be followed by a bonfire and a maybe even a sing-along, if the kids got Cody started, as they always did.

Everyone was in high spirits. Everyone but Kyle.

"Hey, Kyle?"

He dumped the armful of firewood by the pit and turned to Cody. "What?"

It must have come out sharper than he intended because Cody put two hands up in defense. "I guess Stef's not back yet, huh?"

Kyle grunted an answer before reaching for the baby who was crawling toward the ashes of the last bonfire they'd held, months earlier. He hooked a finger under the boy's overalls and lifted him into the air. It was Ty and Lana's younger kid. Amazing how the little guy had grown. At the last bonfire, he'd been a helpless baby. Now he was crawling on all fours. Kind of a miracle, if he thought about it.

He got stuck in the moment, somehow, looking at the child, feeling the wiggle of the tiny body testing his strange new

167

position in the air.

"Thanks!" Lana came running up to take over. She cuddled the child close and turned away, cooing a mild reproach at her son. "What's my little boy doing over here? Daddy needs you over there!"

Kyle stood blinking in her wake, thinking he wouldn't have minded holding the little guy a minute longer. Then he caught Cody giving him one of the knowing looks he excelled at.

He scowled in return and dusted off his hands. The ashes were from the last big event, a send-off for Tyrone, the pack's retired alpha and the father of Ty, Tina, and Cody. With Greer dead, North Ridge needed a strong leader to put the pack in order.

"Should be you, Kyle," Ty had grunted at the time, piercing him with those black-brown eyes. Having killed the North Ridge alpha in a fair fight, it was Kyle's right to take over that pack. It made sense: North Ridge could use a fresh face and steady, quiet leadership to rebuild after years of Greer's oppressive rule.

"You're just what they need," Tina had insisted.

She wasn't the only one. Many of Kyle's packmates—as well as North Ridge wolves relieved to be free of Greer's heavy-handed ways—had urged him to take over.

"Not interested," he had responded, again and again. As much as running a pack appealed to the alpha in him, he had no desire to leave Twin Moon Ranch. For the first time in his life, he felt at home.

Stef understood it best. While others shook their heads and whispered of a missed opportunity, she knew. Neither he nor she was interested in another move.

So old Tyrone, the retired Twin Moon alpha, had headed north to "knock some sense into that disgrace of a pack," as he so delicately put it, and Kyle was secretly relieved. So was everyone else at Twin Moon Ranch. Old Tyrone was a respected leader but not an easy character to have around. Let him go to North Ridge, they nodded to each other, for as long as it might take for a new alpha to emerge. Someone who could run the pack properly.

Kyle had no regrets. He rubbed his hands on his jeans and gauged the wood pile. Still not enough. He turned with a sigh and headed back for another armful just as two kids came hurtling by with a big black dog in slobbery pursuit.

"Cody! Cody!" cried one.

"Daddy! Daddy!" yelled the other, and Kyle recognized Cody's older daughter. Only Cody's kids had hair that shade of blond. That was all the greeting the girls got off before rushing off on whatever mission they were on.

"Hi, sweetie!" Cody called after the kids then caught up with Kyle. "Hey, Tina wanted to know if..." he started then broke off. "I'll ask you later."

Kyle glowered at him. "Why later?"

"Because you're easier to talk to when Stef is home," Cody said with that smile he never extinguished. Everything was funny to Cody, even when the world was dark.

Kyle knew it only seemed dark at this moment; it always felt like that when his mate was away. Deep in his bones, he knew that life was good. Very good. But he was a greedy bastard who wanted his mate around—all the time, if he had his way. Being separated for normal working hours was hard enough, but Stefanie's job sometimes called for overtime. The company had been delighted to have her back once everything settled down and promptly assigned her to their growing Arizona consultancy. She only traveled away a couple of times a month—and never, ever to questionable places. He made damn sure of that. Still, she was away too often for his taste. But what could he do? His job was important, and so was hers. At least he knew she'd be safe now that she'd been marked. As his.

The thought made him stand a little taller, a little prouder. She'd marked him, too, and he fingered the spot now. His favorite scar.

Mine, the wolf growled inside.

He was about to crack a reply to Cody when two arms circled him from behind and a familiar warmth pressed into his back.

He let out a long, relieved breath. "You're home."

Stef kissed the side of his neck and there it was, the sun coursing back into him. "Hmmm," she agreed, "home."

He turned and pulled her into a smothering clinch of a hug—because a kiss would have taken far more coordination than he could muster with his spirit singing the way it was. *Home is wherever you are.*

"Hey, Stef! You're back!" Cody called.

"Hey Stefanie, how was your trip?" Tina asked. She dropped her voice as she brushed by, balancing a tower of paper plates. "Next time make it a little shorter. Make our lives easier, will you?"

Stefanie turned to face him, and although she was pointing an accusing finger at his chest, all he saw for a moment was her eyes: the deep honey-brown he'd always loved. There were sparks of pure gold, too, a permanent mark of her Changeling days, though the gray and green tones had faded away as she settled into her shifter body.

"You haven't been snapping at everyone, have you?"

"Yes!" Tina called over her shoulder.

"No!" Kyle insisted.

"Yes!" Cody yelled.

"Maybe," Kyle grunted, pulling her close again. So he got a little cranky when his mate was away. Was that his fault?

"Hey, Stef," Heather said as she jogged by with water jugs in each hand. "I called you for my team in the soccer game."

"Wait a minute!" Lana chipped in from a few steps away. "Rae and I called her for our team."

"I call her," Kyle growled, and the others laughed and moved on.

"How was your trip?" he whispered then, keeping her close, the line of her body assuring him she really was back.

"It was fine. But you know what?" Her eyes shone with good news. "Remember that condo complex in Sedona I was telling you about? They're going full solar, and we got the contract!"

He found himself hanging on to a breath, wondering if it meant what he hoped.

"So only short trips from now on." She seemed as happy with the news as he was. "For the next couple of months, anyway."

His hopes faded. "What happens after that?"

"I told the company I'd be needing some time off," she said, tucking her chin into the nook by his shoulder. "I think it's finally time for our own home improvement project."

He drew a blank on that one. They already had solar panels on the house and had started installing a solar array on the biggest barn on the ranch. He knew Stef had grand plans for more, but those would be long-term, community projects. So what kind of home improvement did she mean?

"What project?"

"The one you keep harping on," she said, poking his belly.

His heart stuttered. Ever since Greer had introduced the idea of a child, he hadn't been able to erase the image. He'd been carefully feeling his mate out on the topic, but Stef said she wanted to settle in and concentrate on her career for a while longer. Kyle could understand about wanting to prove yourself, so he hadn't pushed it. But if she was really ready...

"You mean, that project?" he managed, poking her back.

The healthy tan of her cheeks went a little pink as she nodded.

"You're sure?"

"I'm sure if you're sure." And Jesus, she really looked sure. Glowing. Happy. His.

"I'm sure!" he blurted.

Stefanie laughed. "Definitely?"

"Definitely."

"Not just possibly?"

He grabbed her finger before she could tease him any more. "Not possibly. Not maybe. Definitely."

"Good," she smiled and pulled him into a kiss. "Because I'm that sure, too." She drew a finger down his cheek and whispered, "Thanks for waiting."

He got lost in her lips for a while, and when his brain clicked back into gear, he had to clear his throat. *Definitely* had more of an effect on him than he expected it to.

Stefanie smiled and swept him into a kiss that had a little more tongue and a lot more heat.

"Hmmm," he murmured, tugging her closer. "How about we get started right now?"

She glanced around. "You mean, *now*, now?"

"Now, now," he grinned, pulling her in the direction of the old bunkhouse. They'd fixed it up for the times they stayed over on the ranch. A home away from home of sorts, and one they were considering fixing up for a permanent move. Living out on the farthest edge of the ranch was gradually losing its appeal. A wolf belonged with his pack, after all.

"The good thing about being part wolf," he started, slinging an arm across her shoulders, "is that you're entitled to take yourself for a walk whenever you want."

Stef wound her hand behind his back and slipped it into the rear pocket of his jeans as they strode away from the others. "Just a walk, huh?"

He held back an answer, because otherwise his lips might move straight into another kiss and they'd never make it to the privacy of the bunkhouse.

They walked to the top of a rise and paused there, taking in the view. The ranch was a flurry of barbecue preparations, but the meandering trail to the old bunkhouse beckoned in the opposite direction. Beyond, the hills rose in layers until they merged with purple mountains far, far away. There was a time when the view had made him feel like an outsider looking in. But not any more. He felt Stefanie's body rise then dip in a satisfied sigh.

Yeah, he knew just what she meant. It was good to be home.

∞∞∞

Other books by Anna Lowe

The Wolves of Twin Moon Ranch

Desert Hunt (the Prequel)

Desert Moon (Book 1)

Desert Wolf 1 (a short story)

Desert Wolf 2 (a short story)

Desert Wolf 3 (a short story)

Desert Blood (Book 2)

Desert Fate (Book 3)

Desert Heart (Book 4)

Happily Mated After (a short story)

Desert Yule (a short story)

Desert Rose (Book 5)

Desert Roots (Book 6)

Serendipity Adventure Romance

Off the Charts

Uncharted

Entangled

Windswept

Adrift

Travel Romance

Veiled Fantasies

Island Fantasies

visit www.annalowebooks.com

Sneak Peek I: Desert Heart

As daughter of the retired alpha, shapeshifter Tina Hawthorne
lives for her pack. She's never been tempted to throw caution
to the wind for a man — until Rick Rivera returns. The sweet
boy from the adjoining ranch is all grown up, but that doesn't
make the irresistible human any more suitable as a mate. Especially with a dangerous new foe haunting the night and Rick
harboring a few secrets — and enemies — of his own.

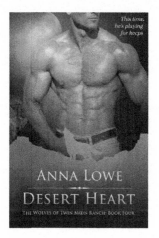

Sneak Peek II: Chapter One

Tina looked out the side window as her brother drove his pickup down the scalloped dirt road. His left hand was clenched white on the wheel; his right, scratching at his ear. She pulled in a long, steadying breath, wishing she could tell her brother to do the same. The way Ty muttered and glared at every bush, it wouldn't surprise her if one of them burst into flames.

"Damn ranch."

He didn't mean Twin Moon Ranch — their home, their legacy. A place their father had toiled over for over a century. The ranch was prospering under the leadership of her two brothers. Twin Moon pack was healthy and expanding, their finances solid, the future promising.

No, Ty wasn't cursing over things at home. He was cursing the neighboring property. Seymour Ranch.

Tina wound a length of her hair around her index finger and tried sending out calm vibes. Ty was just like their father: he hated change, especially when it came to their corner of Arizona. Every stranger, every new face was a cause for suspicion. And in some ways, he was right. Even when things on the ranch ran smoothly, the outside world didn't cease to pose a threat. There was always one danger or another lurking out there. They'd had to fight off rogue shifters twice in recent years, not to mention a vampire intrusion. Tension with rival packs were a constant, too.

She watched a patch of prickly pear blur past, their thorns waving a warning. Trouble was always afoot. The only question was where it would come from next.

"Damn that old bat and her will," Ty continued.

"Ty!" That, she wouldn't stand for. "Mrs. Seymour was a sweet woman. Don't you ever forget how nice she was to us!"

Ty clenched his jaw and wobbled it right, then left — the closest he ever came to retracting his own words. His gaze, though, went softer. He had to remember. The home-baked cookies, the Thanksgiving feasts — or at least, the couple of feasts their father had let them attend before he decided to slam the door shut. The little bit of normalcy they'd lacked after their mother had taken off. Mrs. Seymour always had a gentle smile and soft words for them. For everyone, actually.

"Damn her will, then," Ty muttered.

That, she had to give him. Although Lucy Seymour had passed away several years ago, there were still surprises popping out of her will — or rather, her wills. Because an addendum to the original had recently surfaced. The lawyers had gone over it with a fine-tooth comb and declared it legit. Unusual, but legit.

"Secret heir?" Ty scowled. "What as she thinking?"

"She must have had her reasons." Although for the life of her, Tina couldn't think why Mrs. Seymour would leave everything to a secret heir. The rumor mill was rife with speculation on who that might be, since the Seymours were childless. An illegitimate child, maybe? An old friend? A former lover?

Whoever it was, he or she was keeping a low profile, letting lawyers and the new manager — a person also specified in the will — handle things for now.

"Damn thing, bringing in a new manager out of nowhere," Ty grunted.

"It is odd." Dale Gordon had been foreman of Seymour Ranch for decades. He'd run things capably enough in the period of limbo that followed Lucy Seymour's death. Why rock the boat now? "I bet Dale is delighted."

Ty snorted. "I bet."

She sighed. "Look, we'll be there in another mile. And who knows? Maybe we'll find out the new manager isn't such a bad guy."

Ty grunted. Dale Gordon was no saint, but he was a known quantity, while the new manager was not. And in Ty's mind, a man was guilty until proven innocent.

He did, however, stop scratching his ear long enough to snag one of the cookies Tina held on a plate in her lap.

"Hey!" She slapped at her brother's hand. "Those are for the new manager. Our new neighbor."

"Perfectly good cookies...."

"We're showing that we're friendly."

Ty's scowl etched deep lines on his weathered face.

"You look just like Dad when you do that," she murmured.

He scowled deeper then went through a series of facial contortions to replace it with a look of ferocious displeasure that was uniquely his own. Tina held back a chuckle. Her older brother had spent his entire childhood wanting to be a big bad alpha just like their father, only to realize he wanted to be nothing like the old man at all. He'd softened up a little, Ty had, letting out a little more human and a little less wolf. Mating had been good for him. Parenthood, too. Tina sent out a silent thanks to whatever fate had sent her brother a woman like Lana.

Ty jabbed the cookie in the direction of Seymour Ranch, then shoved it in his mouth. "You planning on buttering the guy up?"

If the front bench of the truck hadn't been so wide, she'd have jabbed an elbow into his ribs. "Definitely not. And it could be a woman for all we know."

Five years ago, Ty might have snorted that comment away, but now he knew better. Another thing he'd learned from his more-than-capable mate.

They drove on in silence. Ty took the last two turns, slowed to coast under the double S brand hanging from the Seymour Ranch gate, then pulled to a halt in front of the homestead. A tall figure separated itself from the shadows of the porch and stepped into sunlight to greet them.

Tina blinked and bit back a gasp.

The new manager was no woman.

The new manager was no stranger.

The new manager was... *Christ, not him.*

More from Anna Lowe

Check out the other side of Anna Lowe with a series even die-hard paranormal fans rave about: the Serendipity Adventure Romance series. You can try it FREE with *Off The Charts*, a short story prequel you can receive for FREE by signing up for Anna Lowe's newsletter at *annalowebooks.com*!

Listen to what a few Twin Moon fans have to say about this new series:

- *This is as HOT as her shifter series. For those who want spicy without paranormal, this is a perfect start. I can't wait to read more about these characters.*

- *I'm enjoying Anna's new series just as much as I do her Wolves of Twin Moon Ranch series.*

- *It's not my normal genre but I do love Anna Lowe's romance books because of the great way she writes. I am really happy this book was the same great style.*

- *Uncharted is different from Anna's Wolves of Twin Moon Ranch but I enjoyed the story just as well.*

About the Author

USA Today and Amazon bestselling author Anna Lowe loves putting the "hero" back into heroine and letting location ignite a passionate romance. She likes a heroine who is independent, intelligent, and imperfect – a woman who is doing just fine on her own. But give the heroine a good man – not to mention a chance to overcome her own inhibitions – and she'll never turn down the chance for adventure, nor shy away from danger.

Ann is a middle school teacher who loves dogs, sports, and travel – and letting those inspire her fiction. Once upon a time, she was a long-distance triathlete and soccer player. Nowadays, she finds her balance with yoga, writing, and family time with her husband and young children.

On any given weekend, you might find her hiking in the mountains or hunched over her laptop, working on her latest story. Either way, the day will end with a chunk of dark chocolate and a good read.

Visit AnnaLoweBooks.com

Made in the USA
Coppell, TX
11 June 2022

78733547R00114